This book is a work of fiction. The names, characters, places, and incidents are products of the writer's imagination or have been used fictitiously and are not to be construed as real. Any resemblance to persons, living or dead, actual events, locale or organizations is entirely coincidental.

There's no hell like a Knight scorned...

The Knights have always assumed little sister Lexi needed to be protected. They were wrong. Lexi knows what she wants and isn't afraid to go after it. And what (or rather *who*) she wants is the sexy sixth man on her brothers' special ops team. She knows he loves her, too. Now, they can *finally* be together. Or, they *could* if he hadn't run off on her...

Matthew Rock has his life together. Or, at least he *did*. But that was before he stepped on a mine and blew himself up, losing an arm and any hope he had of laying claim to Lexi all on the same day. She's been through too much to have to deal with his issues. So, he'll do the right thing and stay away. Even if the *right* thing feels *all* wrong...

Getting to happily ever after with Lexi might be Rocko's toughest — and most rewarding — mission yet. If she can convince her wounded warrior to take it (and her) on, that is...

Angel of the Knight

by

Em Petrova

Chapter One

"Catch ya later, assholes," Matthew Rock called out to the guys of Knight Ops and received two waves, a salute and a middle finger in return.

Laughing as he climbed behind the wheel of his SUV, his back muscle gave a sharp twinge.

Too many hours frozen in the same position, rifle resting on his knee and the sights aimed on the dumb fucker who was trafficking humans. The guy had evaded Homeland Security for more than a year and sent hundreds of women, young men and children into service in the United States as house slaves, sex slaves and worse.

But this time Knight Ops had finally been called in to deal with him, and their special ops unit never failed.

He rolled down the window to drink in some of the cooler breeze coming off the Gulf and backed out of the parking spot on the military base.

"Not if I catch you first, Rocko," his team captain Ben called back.

Rocko threw a wave, and from the corner of his eye, caught a scrap of red on the passenger's seat.

He slammed on the brakes. Lace and silk.

Fuck.

Only one woman would put those panties in his vehicle.

Only one even existed in Rocko's world.

Since realizing his feelings ran deeper for her than anything a one-night stand could provide, he hadn't had a woman in too many months to count. When he'd begun working with the five Knight brothers, he'd never guessed he'd take one look at their baby sister and know she was the woman he wanted for the rest of his life.

Lexi Knight.

L'il sis was guarded like fucking royalty, and every time she got a boyfriend, the guys would hunt him down and warn him off. Of course, Lexi's taste in men sucked—she seemed to gravitate to the worst of the male sex.

But it was also the primary reason Rocko had spent years battling his own desires and shooting down every advance the woman threw his way.

This time, panties.

Red. Silk. Panties.

He tentatively reached across the console and closed his fingers on the smooth fabric, imagining her warmth still clung to the fibers as he drove out of the parking lot and away from any of her brothers who might see him bring the panties to his nose.

He inhaled deeply.

Jesus Christ. They were worn.

The sweet, musky scent of pussy filled his nose and had his cock standing straight up against the fly of his cargo pants.

He lowered the garment, eyes blurred with fantasies of nudging her golden tan thighs apart and opening his mouth over her wet pussy.

God, it was like a drug gift-wrapped in one lace-edged scrap of cloth. Pure torment.

With them gripped in his fist, he brought them back to his nose and inhaled.

The faint trace of Lexi's perfume filled his head. A sort of citrus with underlying notes of flowers.

The woman was going to drive him off the deep end.

His cock head swelled and he felt precum seeping from the tip to wet his briefs.

He had two choices—drive over to the Knights and reach under Lexi's skirt to see if she was bare-assed. Or drive home and ignore her overture to get him into her bed.

What was the worst her brothers could do to him? Kill him and bury him came to mind, but surely they were too good of friends to off one of their team members.

Maiming was another story.

Rocko brought the panties back to his nose. Fuck, she was sweeter than he'd fantasized. How the hell could he ever look at her the same way again?

That was what she was counting on—that he'd scale that wall between her and her brothers like he was storming a fucking fortress. Hell, he couldn't deny he wanted that. One glance down at the bulge in his pants could attest to how much pent-up need he harbored in his very blue balls.

She's off-limits.

Not only because of her overprotective family but Rocko had always known that he was no good for Lexi. He'd never be there enough. She needed—deserved—a man who worked nine-to-five and came home to kiss his wife before dinner and then take her to bed and show her just how much he appreciated her.

What could Rocko offer her besides a lifetime of fearing he would never return home? That if he did, the mission might wear on him. Render him silent.

Sure, he handled stress better than many Marines he'd seen, but he hid a hell of a lot behind his easy smiles too. He stuffed it down, same as when his mother had left him and his sister to be raised by their father.

He was a good dad, did the best he could. But he wasn't around a lot since he worked to support them and that left Rocko in charge.

Now his father was dead and Rocko couldn't even talk to him about any of this.

He opened his fist over the passenger's seat to release Lexi's gift. But before he dropped them, he brought them back to his nose. God, what a fucking pervert he was, but she'd counted on him being enough of one to taunt him into making a move.

As he inhaled deeply, his phone rang.

He dropped the panties into his lap, trying not to think of Lexi's round ass seated there, molded against his steely erection, and answered the cell.

"Rocko."

Ben's voice filled his ear. "Lexi just called. She's got some party for us tonight."

He closed his eyes momentarily. He couldn't trust himself to get within a Louisiana mile of the woman right now, not with her tight curves and sweet pussy on his mind.

"Can't make it," he grated out.

"Bullshit. What do you have planned besides going home and beating off?"

He didn't have any idea how close to the truth that was.

Swallowing, Rocko glanced down at the red panties in his lap. "I can't make it," he said again.

"Lexi won't take no for an answer."

Of course she wouldn't. The woman was relentless—and going to get him beaten to a pulp by her brothers for giving in to her.

If he was smart, he'd toss her panties out the window and drive to his lonely, dull, beige apartment instead of going to the Knights' big, cozy house filled with flowers Lexi brought home to be tormented by the most beautiful, desirable woman in the universe.

Ben went on, "It's some kind of strawberry festival. Now, don't break my little sister's heart. She's far too sweet for the likes of you and the least you can do is show up and eat some shortcake." Ben's words hit like grenades.

She *was* too sweet for the likes of him.

How many times had he considered giving in and taking her? Only knowing he couldn't finish the job and end the fling with her standing before a minister and wearing white had stopped him.

"I already got an invitation," he said huskily. Strawberry-colored panties from the woman herself.

"Good, then see ya there."

Rocko ended the call and fingered the garment in his lap again. Dammit, he didn't have much choice but to go. What then? He couldn't exactly walk in and look at Lexi, knowing she'd given him the panties right off her body. That if he threw her skirt up and bent her over, he could sink balls-deep into her tight pussy.

He let out a heavy sigh and turned the vehicle toward the Knights' place.

Fuck, he was in so much trouble. After battling Lexi's bold advances for the entire past year, Rocko's control was slipping fast and furious.

This time he didn't know if he could stop himself from laying claim to the Knights' sister.

* * * * *

Two years. Lexi Knight had spent two whole years trying to convince that thick-headed man that he not only loved her but couldn't live without her.

She'd also been working to convince him that her brothers wouldn't kill him for making a move on her.

Of course, she didn't know that last part—only figured that since her brothers loved Rocko and worked with him closely on the Knight Ops team, they must like him. So why should they have an issue with him dating her?

Lexi'd tried everything. She'd spent a month leaving Rocko sweet little texts and sending anonymous gifts to him. Coffees in the mornings delivered by a teen neighbor. A bouquet of beef jerky in all flavors from teriyaki to Cajun hot. This time, she'd left her panties on the front seat of his SUV.

For all she knew, Rocko had tossed the coffee down the drain, fed the jerky to a stray dog and threw her panties out the window.

This whole non-love affair would eventually drive her stark-raving mad into the Louisiana swamps. She just knew by that dark, intense look in his eyes that Matthew Rock was in love with her.

The stubborn ass just wouldn't admit it yet.

She chewed the end of her pen and stared into space, not really seeing the flowers she'd just arranged in a beautiful porcelain pot. The kitchen smelled heavenly of baking shortcakes and strawberries she'd just crushed and liberally sugared. Next came the whipping cream, but she couldn't get Matthew off her mind.

It was time for extreme measures.

She'd tried throwing herself at him—landing in his lap wearing nothing but a skimpy bikini. Seeing his pupils dilate as he struggled not to lay a hand on her to even remove her from his lap had given her the only thrill yet.

The man was either a monk or he really just wasn't interested.

What *would* he say about finding her panties in his vehicle? He'd know they were hers, since red was her signature color. If she wasn't wearing it, she had a red rose tucked behind one ear.

She'd tested him before and it had backfired horribly. After many months of being let down by him, she'd run off to get her head on straight. She'd secretly hoped he would chase her and they'd end up in a motel somewhere for days, rolling in the sheets.

Instead, her brother's buddy—and her twin sister's new boyfriend—Bo Hawkeye had been sent after her.

Sure she'd made a good friend in Bo, but she'd been wishing for...

For...

She cocked her head at the sounds coming from outside the kitchen door. She dropped the pen and ran to the sink, leaning to peer from the small window with gauzy white curtains twitching in the sweet Cajun breeze.

Her gaze landed on cars in the drive and her family members piling out. Her brothers and their wives and children. Her sister and Bo were just pulling in.

And trailing behind was Matthew's SUV.

She wondered if he still had her panties stored somewhere, maybe the glove compartment.

Her stomach dropped low and that tingle took up permanent residence whenever he was around.

If she could get him alone, then her morning spent baking and cleaning the house in preparation wasn't for nothing.

With her parents out of town on a short trip to relatives up north, it felt odd to hold a family gathering without them. But this girl was desperate, and how else could she get the man she wanted over here?

Besides, she did have a lot of strawberries to eat herself.

She had to get the whipped cream prepared fast so she had something to entice Matthew with. If she had her way, she'd have the Marine—and the whipped cream—locked in her bedroom.

The kitchen door flew open and her brother Sean and his wife Elise entered, the baby riding on Elise's hip.

Lexi whirled with a grin for all, especially her little nephew who was drooling buckets, his chin and bib damp and his little fist shoved in his mouth.

"Hello, my little doll," she cooed, taking the child. She kissed his soft hair just as more family came through the door. Soon the kitchen was overflowing with people and she had to smack her twin sister Tyler's fingers for trying to steal a shortcake.

Still bouncing the baby on her hip, Lexi was pulled into several conversations at once with her siblings, though she was wholly aware of the last guest to walk into the room.

Matthew Rock, aka Rocko. Sixth man on the Knight Ops team, a division of Homeland Security. The rugged man had an expression that could wipe a man flat even before his bullet did the job.

And from across the room, his gaze landed on Lexi and stole her breath, her mind.

Her heart.

All over again.

She'd been in love with him since the first time she laid eyes on him. She'd also spent a long time wondering if she was even worthy of a guy like him. She was younger and well, she had *problems*.

Though she had many selling points, the lack of oxygen at birth had landed her with a terrible memory for numbers and sometimes her family said she lacked in common sense.

Another reason her siblings were so protective of her. And in her opinion, why they had Matthew too scared to make his move.

At least that was her best guess as to why he avoided her at all costs, yet looked at her the way he was now, like he was undressing her, peeling off the pretty blue dress she wore, easing the straps over her bare shoulders and then her breasts. Finally dropping the cloth over her hips to puddle on the floor.

Her nipples hardened inside the cups of her strapless bra.

"Oooh, there's margaritas," one of her sisters-in-law squealed, going for the glasses already with sugar on the rims.

She broke Matthew's stare and turned to hand off her nephew and get the show on the road so she could hurry up and get to the part where the man she wanted traced a path over her body with a big fat berry dipped in whipped cream and then licked it all off her.

"I'm glad you could all come," she said with a smile.

"Holy crap, Lexi. How many quarts of berries did you buy?" her sister Tyler asked.

"Enough to put up jam for all of us for the season but there was still plenty left over, which is why I thought of a strawberry shortcake and margaritas party."

Her sister-in-law Fleur touched a petal of the red flower in the arrangement. "You should be a party planner, Lexi. You've got such an eye for things and the shortcakes look mouth-watering."

She glanced from the corner of her eye at Matthew. Dressed in faded jeans with a rip in the upper thigh that exposed the white of his pocket and a black T-shirt straining over his muscled chest, *he* was the only mouth-watering thing Lexi could see in the room.

Her libido spiked higher.

She'd been denying herself for months, hoping—praying—that the stubborn ass would finally give in to her advances.

With any luck, her last ploy with her panties had done the trick and today would be the day.

She bustled around the kitchen gathering the last of the items she needed. The white plates and silver flatware were gleaming and the shortcakes piled in a big crock for everyone to grab and dump the fixin's over.

"I just need to quickly whip the cream. It's been chilling in the fridge." As she crossed the room, she was totally aware of Matthew's stare following her. She made a show of bending over to withdraw the big bowl from the shelf.

"Let me help you." His deep voice thundered through her body and hit every speed bump as she looked up into his eyes.

He stood next to her, holding out his hands to take the bowl.

"Thank you." Her voice just came out breathless, as it did often when he was around.

Which was enough to drive her crazy.

When she handed him the bowl, she brushed her fingers over his knuckles.

Usually when she flirted, he smiled at least. Not today. His somber expression had her equally turned on and on high alert. What was going on with him?

He carried the bowl to the counter. She shot him a smile but didn't get one in return. He just went back to leaning against the wall, watching her.

She whipped the cream. Everyone chatted and teased each other. Tyler succeeded in stealing that shortcake and cramming it whole into her mouth before Lexi could stop her.

Then everything was ready and people made an assembly line to get their treats. Piled high with whipped cream and white chocolate shavings for some, the shortcakes were a hit.

Then the margarita blender was fired up and pretty soon the gathering shifted to full party mode.

Carrying a bowl and a glass outside to the patio, Lexi tossed a beckoning glance over her shoulder at Matthew.

His eyes drilled into her.

A little shaken by that look, she set her dish and drink on the patio table and smoothed her skirt over

13

her behind as she sat, aware she was bare beneath the full skirt and aching for Matthew.

After a minute he joined her at a small table in the shade.

Lexi sent the hunky special ops guy a lingering look as he took the seat next to her. *What are you waiting for?* she wanted to ask him. But she just dug her spoon through layers of white chocolate, whipped cream, strawberries and shortcake.

"Glad you could come," she said, taking the bite.

He watched her. Then he raised his glass which was all rum and not a splash of strawberry to be seen.

Uh-oh.

"Matthew, what's going on?"

He lifted a shoulder in a shrug. "Why do you think something's going on?"

"Day drinking? That's not like you."

"You're day drinking too." He lifted his angular jaw toward her fruity drink.

"It's mostly strawberry and syrup."

His gaze locked on her mouth. She'd never seen him so intense and couldn't pick apart the knot he had firmly tied her insides into.

She lowered her spoon and ran her tongue over her lower lip. "Do I have whipped cream on my face?"

He gave a rough shake of his head. "You know damn well what you're doing to me, Lexi."

14

Her mouth fell open on a small puff of air. For all their dancing around each other, he'd never been so blunt. She must have finally gotten under his skin.

"You're worrying me. Did something happen during the last mission?" She sat back in the wood chair to study him.

He was unchanged, other than the lack of a smile on his handsome face. He was always easygoing and this... this wasn't him. Maybe he was angry with her for testing him.

He blew some air through his nostrils. "Last mission was to be expected. No surprises, just handled things."

"I know sometimes those 'things' can be upsetting. Wear you down. Do you need to talk?"

He looked her straight in the eyes. His stare deep, penetrating. "I realized some things while I was fighting for our country."

She swallowed, the miniscule strawberry seeds seeming to catch in her throat. "What's that?"

His deep brown eyes the color of rich coffee drilled into her.

"That I don't have anything to come home to."

She opened her mouth, but he cut across her before she could form words.

"Tell me about the flower shop."

The jump in topic had her spinning. She blinked and to cover her confusion, she took another bite of shortcake. Tasting nothing.

She mulled over his question. She had a special love for the flower shop where she worked. Learning about all the blooms, creating beautiful things for people's special days, always thrilled her. But last week she'd made an error with the register that had earned her an ear blistering from her boss.

It was beyond frustrating for her to know her shortcoming was with numbers and not be able to do anything about it. She had the steps all written out to follow each time she rang out a customer. But she still made mistakes.

She couldn't admit any of this to Matthew, though. And telling her family was out of the question. They already gave her that 'poor Lexi' look each time her 'problem' was brought up.

She pushed out a sigh and shook her head. "Work is fine. I love my job."

Just not when she was goofing up and getting chewed out.

Matthew contemplated her, the set of his shoulders more tense somehow. What had she said to set him off and plant that crease between his brows?

He raised his glass and drained the last drops of rum. Watching him, warmth slid low in her belly, gripping at every female part in its path.

Whatever was going on with the man she wanted, he wasn't giving away any secrets. Only thing she knew was that he was changed. The air was loaded.

And she wanted him—right now—and with a burning need that made her past desire seem like a teenage crush.

* * * * *

That stubborn set of Lexi's jaw set him off even as the vulnerable pout of her lips had him wondering what the hell she was hiding from him.

Times like these, Matthew didn't consider himself the rock she needed to cling to. And that was exactly what he wanted to provide for the rest of her life, but if her family couldn't get her to lean on them, he didn't have a prayer.

Dammit, he'd wanted her for years. Dreamed about her every fucking night when he fell into bed, bruised and battered, sometimes lucky to walk away with his life after a deadly mission. And every waking minute in between.

So many things held him back, including her brothers sitting just inside feasting on strawberry shortcake.

The one time her brother Dylan had caught him talking to her alone, he'd warned him to steer clear or end up with a combat boot planted up his ass. If anybody else had warned him off a woman, Rocko would have told him to fuck off. But he had to work with the Knights—their every move must be matched. And therefore, no strife could come between them.

17

Sadness touched the corners of her beautiful pouty lips painted in a deep red hue that flattered her skin so well. What he really wanted was to see that lipstick smeared, messed up from his kisses.

Everything about her reminded Matthew of a pinup girl. And recently he'd been thinking about adding another tattoo to his collection of body art. He had a spot on his ribs just begging for some ink of his baby.

Only she wasn't his.

Though she made it quite clear with her come-to-bed eyes and each twitch of her curves that she wanted to be.

She'd made it more than clear that if he made an advance, that she'd open up her heart to him. Not to mention her body.

Damn, he could almost smell her on those slinky panties.

She shot him little covert glances, nervously chewing her lower lip. Did she realize she'd pushed him too far?

"Matthew…"

She rarely called him by his first name—no one did besides his sister. Damn, she was pulling out all stops today, taking their relationship to a deeper, more intimate level all around.

He dipped his finger into the whipped cream dollop on top of his shortcake and sucked it off. She watched with as much enthrallment as he'd expected.

Had she put on any panties? Back in the kitchen, he'd stared at her ass and couldn't detect any panty lines.

"Matthew, I fear you must be angry with me."

He dropped his palms to the table, gripping the edge to keep from grabbing her, bending her over his arm and kissing the sweetness right off her lips. Sliding his hand under her dress and locating the source of her delicious scent.

She dropped her fork and stared at him. "I-I'm sorry about what I left in your SUV."

He pushed out a harsh breath.

From inside, he heard the voices of the men he worked with almost on a daily basis. He measured their distance and guessed at how occupied they were with their wives and children.

Would they even notice if he stole away with their sister and didn't return for a long time?

Lexi leaned forward, big eyes wide. "Forgive me, please. I shouldn't have —"

He pushed back from the table and stood. Grabbing her by the forearm, he lifted her to a stand and then he strode across the patio to reach another back door that led in through the garage.

He slid his hold down to her wrist. Beneath his fingertips, her pulse tripped and raced as he led her back into the house and up the stairs.

"Which room's yours?" His question was stupid since he knew as soon as he spotted the floral nightmare covering one bed. Curtains, bedding, a floral-upholstered chair. And a pot of daisies on a white desk.

He dragged her inside a few steps and then quietly closed the door so only they'd hear the click of the lock.

She stood in front of him, trembling. Her dark hair was swept over one shoulder and a full, gorgeous rose tucked behind her ear.

He reached for it, easing it from the strands and then bringing it to his nose. Her chest rose and fell, her cleavage begging for his lips from the V-neck of her dress.

"Matthew, I don't understand what's going on. Are you upset with me?"

He raked his gaze down over her. "Yes. I think you deserve a spanking for what you pulled. For making my cock rock hard the entire way over here. Even now." He took her hand and placed it flat over his fly.

She gasped.

He swept in. Cupping her jaw, he tipped her head up for his kiss. When their lips collided, every fucking thing that had ever been wrong in his life fell into place. All at once, nothing mattered but this stunning, desirable woman in front of him.

She gasped again under his lips and he swept his tongue inside, gathering more flavors to stockpile in his memory for when this was all over and he could no longer have her.

She slipped her arms around his neck, clinging, her body bowed as he landed a hand on the small of her back and forced her to fit him.

Though he didn't have to do much forcing—she just fit. Locked in his hold, kissing him back with everything she had in her.

He tore away. "Your panties drove me wild. I need to touch you. Taste you." There was no taking his time. The clock was counting down and her brothers would eventually come looking for them.

He yanked up her dress, cradling her sleek, bare pussy in his palm.

Dizzy with need, he groaned. She was soaking wet and ready for him.

"Oh God, Matthew," she burst out.

He swallowed her words on a kiss, bearing her backward until she was spread out on the floral hell of a bedspread. Funny thing was, it fit her feminine traits so perfectly that he hadn't imagined anything else.

Breaking the kiss, he stared down into her eyes. "I've fucking wanted you for years, Lexi. I can't have you. But I can have this once."

She dug her nails into his shoulders as he slipped down her body, scraping his unshaven jaw between her breasts. What he wouldn't give to strip her bare and really attend to her the way she deserved, but there wasn't time.

Poised between her thighs, he closed his eyes on the warm scent of her arousal, muskier, earthier than what had been on her panties.

He gripped her by the hips and lifted her to meet his tongue.

The first taste was heaven and hell rolled into one delicious flick of his tongue. The second, he growled out his need and the third she thrust upward for more.

Fuck, he was in so much trouble.

At least if her brothers killed him, he'd die a happy man, with her taste in his mouth.

Chapter Two

Every nerve ending in Lexi's body was a live wire of electricity. How long had she been dreaming of this very moment, and now Matthew was here, touching her.

He splayed his callused fingers across her inner thighs, parting her for more access, and just the sight of his dark head buried between her legs had her gulping back small cries of pleasure.

The burn in her core grew hotter until she squeezed her eyes on the bliss to hold it in longer. All these months of aching, she'd grown to love the build-up but right now she felt the tight rein on her control slipping with each small flick of his tongue.

Sliding wet and warm from hole to clit and back down through her slick, swollen folds.

Her need mounted, and she bit down on her lower lip. Downstairs, the party she'd organized rolled on without her playing hostess, but it was only a matter of time before someone came looking for her.

She dug her fingers into his shoulders and bucked upward as he teased a circle around her clit without really touching down on where she wanted his tongue most. When she opened her eyes, she found Matthew's dark gaze pinning her flat to the bed.

"You're so goddamn beautiful," he murmured, swiping his tongue across his juice-damp lips.

"Take me, Matthew," she whispered.

He lowered his mouth to her pussy again, sucking her clit between his lips hard enough to make her jolt. She sank her fingers into his hair and rode his tongue like she did in every fantasy of them coming together.

Pressure mounted with each stroke, and that coarse hair all over his jaw provided the tingles she'd been craving from the man... well, forever. She'd just known he'd be a giving lover, and she wasn't wrong.

With small sucking pulls of his mouth, he drew her need to the surface. She quaked, belly muscles dipping harshly as she struggled to control the noises she made.

When he eased his fingertip into her pussy and probed the other against her netherhole, she hiccupped as ecstasy bolted through her.

"Oh God. Don't stop," she rasped.

He sank his finger into her pussy and gently entered her backside with only a tip. She stopped breathing at the foreign touch. He wiggled his fingertip and tongue simultaneously.

Suddenly, her body tightened, every sensation converged into one small point of blinding light, and then she shot over the cliff of pleasure.

She cried out as her inner muscles clamped down, convulsing swift and powerful, harder than she ever had come in her life.

Matthew groaned as he lapped at her seam, drawing out her swallowed moans until her inner thighs quivered and she collapsed to the mattress.

When she opened her eyes, it was to find him standing at the end of the bed between her spread legs, strong hands working open his leather belt. The veins snaking down his arms seemed more pronounced and when she flicked her gaze up to his, she found the intensity in his eyes tenfold.

She had no words—they were snatched away as she watched a beautiful man undress in front of her. When his fly hung open to reveal tight black knit fabric barely harnessing the thickness of his erection, he reached between his shoulder blades and pulled his T-shirt overhead.

A puff of air left her lungs. She'd seen him shirtless before, when he came to the cabin and swam in the bayou, dunking her brothers in good fun. One time he'd caught a small gator barehanded and swam with it to the dock, where he placed the creature, who sat there glaring mad.

But seeing the strip show up close and personal— all for her—was something altogether different.

Carved ridges of muscle banded his torso, and above that his pecs were blocks of granite. Both bore tattoos, which she'd also taken a lot of covert looks at from beneath her lashes on a sunny day in the bayou.

But now she would get to touch him, run her fingers over the inky lines of military tattoos and oaths for country and freedom.

Love welled up in her and overflowed, stronger than it had been an hour ago. Intimacy had brought them even closer, and now…

He bent to unlace his boots and then pushed his jeans down, revealing that thick muscle riding just above his hips. The lines that had her mouth watering to lick for hours before throwing her leg over his broad body and sliding down over his length.

She reached for him.

He shed the rest of his clothes quickly and slicked a condom onto his impressive length in one stroke of his fist.

A shiver of anticipation ran through her.

"I want to take my time with you, Lexi. You deserve it." His voice was pitched low. "But I've been waiting so damn long that I can't hold back another second."

He lowered himself over her body, and with a hand under her nape, lifted her to his kiss. She bowed against him, drinking in his masculine flavor and wrapping her thighs around him.

He guided his cock to her entrance. They broke away and stared into each other's eyes. The moment stretched.

And then he claimed her in one long plunge.

She splintered around him, stretching perfectly to fit his shape. The wide girth of him filling her completely and the bulging head seated deep in her core.

Her head dropped back, and he kissed her throat, stamping words there with every brush of his lips. "So hot. Tight. God, yes. I've wanted you forever, baby doll."

Passion threaded through her, and she tightened her grip on the man she wanted more than the next breath of air she took. She rose to meet his thrusts, feeling his muscles bulge and piston with each move he made.

When he changed rhythm, all at once, she was clinging to the cliff of ecstasy again. Her insides fluttered around his cock. He sank balls-deep.

Withdrew.

Staring into her eyes, he issued a long, low groan and unloaded with sharp jerks of his hips.

Under the intensity of seeing him come apart for her, she burst with a cry of her own. Need overruled, and she found Matthew's lips for long, dizzying moments.

He rolled off her, dragging her up against his big body where she felt safe and more loved than she ever had in her life.

His stare skipped over her features and back up to her eyes as if he was branding her on his memory. As long as she lived, she'd never forget their first time together. When they were ninety and smiling at each other toothlessly across their mush dinner, she'd remember this moment and still want him.

She brushed the thick hair out of his blazing eye. "Matthew... I love you. I've loved you for so long."

His chest swelled with a breath of air he didn't release. His eyes closed on her words. She studied the scar through his right brow and another more ragged one on his cheekbone, a small spot where he'd been burned by a piece of burning shrapnel. And a bullet graze riding across his upper biceps.

The man was a walking hero with all the markings to prove it.

When he opened his eyes, he looked straight at her and gave her the words she'd been aching to hear forever.

"Lexi, I love you with my whole heart." He took her hand and placed her palm over the pounding organ beneath his warm chest.

Emotion spilled over in her, and tears sprang to her eyes. She leaned her forehead against his jaw and twisted her hand up to grip his fingers.

She'd never been happier. She was going to marry Matthew Rock and be at his side through thick and thin till death did they part.

At last.

* * * * *

"Goddammit!" Ben screamed into the comms unit until Rocko's eardrums vibrated. "Secure the fucking site!"

"We're fucking trying, bro," came one of the Knight brother's much calmer reply.

Rocko hunkered down behind a dirt embankment, the train tracks in plain sight. The terrorist cell had enough weapons and explosives in this Alabama county to take them off the map. They'd already succeeded in blowing up two government offices in a month, and Knight Ops was fucking ending it here and now.

"Two hundred yards east," Rocko said to Dylan, hunching next to him.

They'd made their move the minute it was too dark to see, but everything was crystal clear through their NVG. The night vision goggles provided high-def proof that they were sitting in the worst possible spot.

"The assholes knew we were coming," Dylan said.

"No shit," Rocko shot back. They were locked down on the fringes of the site, with train cars separating them from Ben and the others. He and Dylan could handle themselves, but something else was concerning.

"Place fucking reeks of Semtex." Rocko stared at the device in his hand that detected plastic explosive, and it was hanging heavy in the air. "I'd bet my new

SUV that nobody's using the compound to blast out a new well in the vicinity." He looked to Dylan. "We gotta get out of here, circle around and meet up with the others."

Dylan peeked over the rise and fell back as shots flew over his head.

"Fucking get the fuck outta there," Ben yelled into their ears.

"Fucking trying, asshole." Dylan bent over into a crouch and booked it.

Rocko was on his heels, swinging his head right and left to watch for ambush and the source of all the explosive. He couldn't detect a damn thing and shit was not going as planned.

He set down his boot.

The explosion rocked him. He landed hard on his side with dirt raining down around him.

His scattered mind honed in on the only thing it could. *It sounds like popcorn.*

A roar came, and he realized it was projecting into his ear through the comms.

Then beside him from Dylan.

"Hold on, man. Jesus Christ!"

Rocko tried to push onto his back but he felt like a crumpled doll. His limbs askew. Where the fuck was he?

Shock was setting in, he thought with a detached calmness.

"Rocko's down! We need evac *now*." That came from Dylan.

Rocko cracked an eye but his night vision goggles had flown off his face in the blast. It was dark, and only a shadow hovered over him.

The sickening tang of blood hit his nostrils. He worked his mouth.

"Shhh, man, don't try to speak. I've got you. I've got you." Dylan rested his gloved hand on the top of Rocko's head. Pain shot through his scalp. He realized he was cut and his teammate was staunching the blood flow.

"Get here motherfucking now!" Dylan yelled.

Rocko tried to push up but his arm wouldn't work. He twisted. Pain was a deep stab that kept him down. He tried again.

"No no no no, stay down. You can't get up, Rocko." Dylan's words sounded far away. "We've got severe injuries and shrapnel. Secure the site. Get him the fuck out!"

Rocko looked up at his buddy but couldn't make out his features, only a rounded hump of his helmet. Where was his own headgear? Blown off? He tried to reach for it but his arm was useless.

He opened his mouth to ask Dylan to find it but nothing came out.

"Hold on, man. No, don't get up."

Using his ab muscles, he leaned forward but a hand pressed him down again. Dirt smelled bad here. Or maybe that was his blood.

Suddenly other hands were on him.

"Hold him down. Chaz, get a tourniquet on his arm."

Rocko succumbed to the black wave washing over him but as soon as someone yanked his arm, so hard it felt as if it was severing from his body, he reared up, swinging with his good arm at whoever was hurting him.

"Hold him down, goddammit." Ben barked the order and Rocko was pinned to the earth again.

"Northeast," he heard someone say into a radio. Coordinates were given.

"How... bad is it?" Rocko managed to say, though his voice sounded rough.

"Check the neck. Get that bleeding stopped," Ben ordered.

More hands touching things that probably should hurt if Rocko could make his brain connect with his body.

Ben stared into his eyes, and Rocko realized for the first time just how much his eyes looked like his sister's. Lexi. She was going to kill him when she found out he was hurt.

He stared up at Ben and imagined his angel leaning over him instead of his captain.

"Jesus. Hold on, Rocko. We're getting you the fuck outta here."

"My... arm."

"We got you under control. Don't worry about anything, you got it?"

That hand was pressing down on his head, and it fucking hurt. The blackness loomed again, wiping Lexi out of his vision and his ears filled with the sound of popcorn again.

Not popcorn.

A chopper.

His world went sideways as someone rolled him over, taking his stomach with it. He swallowed bile and realized his lips were wet with blood too.

"Get him flat. Hurry. Someone have a way to ventilate him?"

Rocko didn't recognize the voices anymore, but he did understand they were being shot at.

Someone from his team unloaded their weapon a few feet from him, and Rocko tried to reach for his own but couldn't lay a hand on it.

"No no no, hold still." Dylan again.

"Got him? Lift." Ben's voice boomed out, giving Rocko the first edge of fear in the tone.

He rose in the air on a backboard and then Lexi's eyes were in front of him again.

No, not Lexi. Ben.

His captain rested a hand on his chest, over his heart. "Guts and glory, man. You were an ugly motherfucker before but now you're really ugly."

Rocko pushed out a chuckle that sounded as a gurgle in the back of his throat.

Ben tapped his chest lightly. "You'll be all right."

"Tell... Tell Lexi I love her," Rocko said. But he was being carried away, toward the noise of the chopper blades. And his men were in the thick of a battle that he would not participate in. He would not be standing guard at their six, prepared to take lives to save his team's.

A tear rolled down his cheek, but he couldn't lift a hand to wipe it away.

Then he heard the word of one of the medics over the radio.

A word that wiped out his whole world.

"Amputee."

Chapter Three

Lexi fiddled with the blooms in the arrangement, moving one here, directing some greenery there. She hummed as she worked, but her mind wasn't on the flowers.

Several feet away in the back room of the shop, her boss was going over the books. He didn't used to look over every single transaction but since her error, he'd started digging deeper and found more mistakes.

The whole ordeal made her stomach hurt, the same as when she'd have a math test in school. Some mornings she'd even throw up and her brothers and sister would have to rally her morale, convince her she could pass the test.

But even being in low level mathematics, she struggled. And often failed.

She threw a look over her shoulder toward the back room. Yep, it was the same. Sitting on pins and needles as the teacher graded her paper and just waiting to see that frown on her face. Only this was her job. Her livelihood.

The pay wasn't all that but she loved what she did, and she couldn't lose this position. Somehow, she had to get her shit together and quit making errors.

On the counter, her phone vibrated with a text from Tyler.

Family meeting. Ben's birthday coming up. The big 3-5.

Lexi pushed out a sigh. She was always up for a party but wasn't feeling that festive at the moment. Besides, all the work fell on her and she wanted to keep her schedule cleared for when Rocko returned.

After their lovemaking, she hadn't heard from him at all. It was understandable—his position with the Knight Ops team kept him away a lot and on a moment's notice. All week long, though, she'd found herself daydreaming of the man.

The way he looked at her.

The way he touched her…

She picked up her phone and thumbed a response to Tyler. *As soon as the guys come home, we can meet.*

Her answer came immediately. *They are home.*

Lexi's heart did a triple backflip and stuck the landing. Her pulse raced out of control at the thought of seeing Matthew again.

Tyler's words flashed across the screen. *Wait, I guess they're out again. Bo just told me.*

And just like that, Lexi's hopes plummeted.

She bit her lower lip and stared at the beautiful fresh flowers in front of her face, trying to focus on something besides her deep ache for the man she loved. Who'd declared his love to her too.

Warmed by the memory she clutched tight to her chest, she finished the bouquet and placed the card in a prominent spot. *Congratulations on your 25th anniversary,* it read.

She teared up.

Someday this would be her bouquet, and she and Matthew would be still just as in love.

Her boss came out of the back room. Eric Young was late-fifties and wore glasses down the bridge of his nose like a much older man. When he looked at her the way he was now, Lexi was always reminded of a disapproving owl.

Usually that amused her and she'd have a chuckle over it in private. But not today.

He held a sheaf of receipts in his hand along with a computer printout.

"How did you make out?" she asked in a voice that was brittle with false cheer.

He planted his feet and stared over his wire rims at her, light blue eyes pinning her down.

She fidgeted in her high heels.

"Lexi, it isn't good news."

"It isn't?" Her mouth was suddenly dry.

"Three more discrepancies in these receipts."

Three? Oh God. She'd be fired. Then she'd be stuck at home until she found another job, listening to

37

her parents bicker and scrubbing the whole house just to have something to do.

She'd have more time to worry over Matthew.

Her boss was staring at her as if waiting for some explanation, which she didn't have.

"I'm sorry for the mistakes, Eric. I'll slow down and be more careful going forward."

He peered at her. "I can't let this continue. You know that, Lexi."

"Of course." She twisted her fingers until they were about to snap off.

"Next time I'll have to write you up for it."

She nodded. She knew he was doing her a favor, that if she hadn't worked here as long as she had, that he'd just can her and hire someone more competent. She also remembered the contract terms—that after a written warning, she had ninety days of probation. One more misstep and she'd basically fire herself.

She pushed out a breath to try to calm down. How was she going to keep from making errors? She knew herself well enough to know she couldn't. Dammit, why did she have to get saddled with this problematic brain of hers?

As always when feeling self-pity, she reminded herself that many were far worse off. She had all her faculties, could function as a normal, healthy person because she was one, if a little slow with math.

"I will have my niece in for more hours too."

Oh God. The worst. Lexi hated working with Eric's niece, Ella. She was lazy and stood around filing her nails, letting Lexi do all the work, until her uncle came in. Then she was super-helpful and sweet as pie.

Of course, he could mean he'd just be giving Ella a bigger cut of her hours and Lexi wouldn't be working with her at all.

"The bouquet looks perfect. Just don't mess up when you ring up the order." Eric gave her a nod and then moved to the back room once more.

She bit her lip at the backhanded compliment and bowed her head.

The rest of her day, her mind was thick with worry and anxiety. Each time someone came into the shop to purchase roses for a girlfriend or an arrangement for a sick parent, she triple-checked her numbers on the receipt and then worried nonstop whether she'd done it right until the next customer came in.

If only the system was automated rather than having an ala carte feature where she was required to list items plus their costs correctly and then add them up.

By the end of the day, she was wrung out, mentally exhausted. All the way home, she replayed her transactions, praying they were correct.

Looking forward to a good Cajun meal and a long, hot bath, she walked through the back door of her family home and stopped in her tracks when heard Ben's voice.

Lexi poked her head into the living room and glanced around, seeing only her mother sitting with her feet propped on a low stool, a magazine in her hands. "Was that Ben I just heard?"

Her *maman* looked up. "Yes, it was."

"He's back then? Tyler said Knight Ops was out again."

Maman shifted her attention to the magazine she held.

"Where did Ben go?"

"Uh, he had something to do. Maybe he just stopped in before his mission," she muttered.

"What is going on?"

Her mother turned her gaze onto Lexi. "He had to run, honey."

She might not have a good handle on anything to do with balancing a checkbook or figuring out the price of a dress if it was twenty-five percent off, but she could read people in a blink. And her *maman's* voice held a note of brightness that made her think she wasn't being straight with her. Not to mention the wary light in her eyes.

If Ben was around, then so was Matthew.

If that man was back to evading her, she was going to spit nails — right at him.

She strode back to the kitchen, pulled out her cell phone and shot off a text to Matthew. As she hit send, she stood there tapping the toe of her red high heel on the tile floor. Something was up, and they were all in on it.

First Tyler saying they were back then no, they weren't. Next her *maman* and Ben too. It could only mean that somehow they'd all found out about her and Matthew and they were keeping him from her.

Anger erupted as she stared at the screen and got no reply. Ten minutes later she was in her car again, halfway to Ben's place. By the time she arrived, she'd chewed her nails to stubs and worn off most of the nail polish drumming them on the steering wheel.

She made the turn onto the long driveway leading to the country home—and immediately knew without a doubt she was being lied to.

God, that pissed her off more than anything. Why did they all believe her to be some little weakling who couldn't handle the truth? Let them try to keep her from the man she loved—who loved her too. Love didn't work that way, and they'd overcome whatever hurdles her family threw in their paths—together.

And if it's Matthew throwing out the hurdles?

Her stomach dropped at that thought and she quickly conjured the way he'd looked down at her after they'd made love that day. Like she was the only thing in his world.

She wasn't poor little Lexi who needed to spend her life standing behind her bodyguard of Knights.

41

By the time she got out of her car and stormed up to Ben's front door, she was fuming. She rapped hard and Dahlia answered, her rounded baby bump peeking around the door before the woman's pretty face.

"Lexi." She threw a look over her shoulder and said louder, "Lexi, what are you doing here?"

She shoved past her sister-in-law into the cozy house decorated in what could only be called rustic elegance. "Where's my brother?"

"He's…"

Ben came out of nowhere, at ease, hands in pockets. And not wearing his cammies.

Lexi glared at his attire. "There's no mission. Why are you evading me? Why is everyone lying to me?"

"We're on call, on hold," he said.

She narrowed her eyes and planted her hands on her hips. "You might be able to lie to everyone from your own *papa* to terrorists, Benjamin Bartholomew Knight, but I know that look in your eyes. You're not being straight with me. Now tell me what the hell's going on."

A baby's wail came from the other room, and he and Dahlia exchanged looks. "I'll get her," Dahlia said softly and scuttled from the room as fast as her pregnant body could go.

Lexi looked into her big brother's eyes and arched a brow. "Well? I'm waiting."

"We're on hold. I told you. Now quit making demands and go on home."

"As soon as you heard me come into our parents' place, you beelined it outta the house. What were you talking to *Maman* about?"

He gave a nonchalant shake of his head that, again, might fool one of the criminals he was trying to snow over, but she knew him better.

"You found out about me and Rocko and you ran him off."

The words were out before she could think twice about saying them.

They fell into the space between her and Ben like lead bricks.

He shifted his gaze to hers, eyes distant and cold in a way she'd never seen directed at her before. She raised her chin a notch. "I love him, and he says he loves me. You won't stop it from happening, Ben. Not you, Sean, Chaz, Dylan or Roades. Not even Tyler, who I know is in on this..." she waved a hand in the air, "conspiracy or whatever you wanna call it. Operation Keep-Lexi-from-Rocko. None of you can stop me from being with him."

She spun and stomped out the door. From behind, Ben called, "Where are you going?"

"To find Matthew, dammit. Since you won't tell me anything, then I'll go looking until I find him myself."

As she reached the car, she glanced back to see Ben standing in the doorway, clutching the frame as if holding himself up.

Angrier than she'd been since she could remember, she spun out of the gravel driveway and hit the main road that would carry her to the man she loved.

Nothing could tear her away from him, especially not her damned overprotective, irritating, interfering family.

* * * * *

"Mr. Rock, let's see how you're looking today."

Rocko turned his face to the window of the cramped hospital room, ignoring the doctor. He'd seen enough of men in white coats, nurses in scrubs and all the white bandages wound around his body for a lifetime.

The doctor moved around the bed and into his line of vision. "I need to examine you, Mr. Rock. I've had a report from the head nurse that you've been combative. Can you explain to me why you wouldn't want them to help you? You can't heal from your injuries without help."

"Fuck off," he said in a flat tone.

Ignoring his outburst, the doctor drew the stethoscope from around his neck. "I just need you to sit forward so I can listen to your lungs."

"No."

44

The doctor looked toward the door and Rocko followed his stare. Ben and Sean stood there.

When were they going to get the hint and stop coming?

He turned his face back to the window. The blinds were drawn and only small chinks of light came through, alerting him that it was day. What day it was, he couldn't say. He didn't give a fuck anymore.

Ben and Sean came forward, boots strangely quiet on the floor, but his acute hearing still worked and he could measure the distance between them and the bed.

"Lean forward please, Mr. Rock." The doctor waited patiently.

He reclined against the hospital bed, not looking at the doctor, his buddies and especially not at the bandages covering what was left of his arm. For the three days since he'd regained consciousness, he'd been ignoring the fact that half of it was missing. He couldn't look at the stump.

"All right, let's discuss your vitals," the doctor said, taking up his chart.

"Let's not."

"You're not taking the painkillers. Any reason why you think playing hero is to your benefit right now?"

"I don't like being foggy." Though he hurt like hell, it was true.

45

"You must have an extremely high pain tolerance."

He grunted.

"All right, then we need to discuss your elevated temperature."

He stared at the cracks of light seeping through the blinds, feeling the last of his reserves trying to drain away. He had enough medical training to know that fever meant infection. And only one thing could be infected.

The heat in his arm was enough to tell him something wasn't right.

From the corner of his eye, he saw the doctor look to his friends.

Ben came forward and Sean sank to the edge of the bed near his feet. "Man, we just want you healthy and whole. You've gotta start listening to what the doctors say. Take your pain meds, do what the nurses tell you," Sean said.

He didn't reply.

"Mr. Rock, last time I examined that arm, I thought it might require another surgery. Several more actually."

"No."

He went on without missing a beat. "It's my belief that the arm needs to come off completely, that it can't be salvaged below the shoulder. We discussed this last time I came in to examine you."

Rocko almost snorted. Last time, he'd sent the doc running for the protection of the hallway.

The doctor reached for the thick bandage to have a look, and Rocko snapped out his good hand, crushing his fingers on the man's wrist.

He issued a low cry.

Ben made a grab for Rocko. "Stop it, Rocko. That's an order!"

Using the last of his strength, he dragged the doctor across the bed so he could glare right into his eyes, same as he would an enemy. "You're. Not. Taking. My. Arm." His voice deadly.

"Rocko, now, goddammit," Ben bit off.

What the hell did he have to lose? He couldn't be part of Knight Ops any longer—Ben wasn't his captain anymore. He was a worthless bag of skin lying in this bed wasting away. Couldn't serve his country, fight, shoot...

Couldn't put both arms around Lexi.

He shoved the doctor away from him, and Ben steadied the man so he didn't fall over. Rocko returned to staring at the slashes of light, feeling it resembled his own chest, flayed open, his blood showing through the gashes the same way the yellow sunlight tried to sneak into this goddamn room.

It seemed the doctor would only go so far in the name of helping a patient. He straightened his lab coat and walked out. A second later, two orderlies entered.

Rocko narrowed his eyes.

Here he'd thought all the fight was out of him, but he was wrong. He had plenty more.

He took a swing at one. The other pinned him down and Ben's face loomed over his as a nurse added a syringe of something to his IV. His eyes drooped on a blink.

"I'm sorry, man, but it's for your own good. You're better off with no arm than dead from gangrene." Ben's voice sounded muffled.

Sean's face loomed over his brother's shoulder. "It's not the end of your career. There are high-tech prosthetics. Keeps you in active duty."

"Fuck," he said thickly as the drugs stole through his system. "It's not that. It's Lexi." A hot tear rolled from the corner of his eye.

Ben's head hung. "Dude, she's going crazy wanting to know what's going on. I'm going to tell her what happened so at least she can be here."

"No," he tried to bark out with all the strength he could muster, but his voice came out as a pitiful whisper. "She can't know. She can't see me like this."

"If she loves you like we think she does, then she won't care. She'll only want to support you," Sean said.

"She can't know." The meds took over his mind and he closed his eyes just as he felt the bed rolling out the door with him on it. Helpless. Hopeless.

He was going to lose his entire arm.

Chapter Four

Pop music played low over the radio in the flower shop, but Lexi hardly heard the strains. She barely registered the deep aroma of the pink roses that had just arrived today, even though she was surrounded by them.

She shook herself for the third time that morning since coming in to work. She was far too distracted, and that could only end with her making yet another mistake with numbers.

"Lexi."

Lexi stared unseeingly at the flowers in her hand and wondering what to do about Rocko. She'd been by his place four or five times and found the windows dark and the blinds drawn. She'd gone to Sean's and he wasn't home either, so she'd begged Elise for information and gotten nowhere. Her sister-in-law was as hard-nosed as her husband when it came to doling out intel.

The longer Lexi went without seeing Matthew, the more confused she became. Was he avoiding her or was her family guarding him from her?

She'd spent a lifetime being petted and protected, and sometimes she admitted she was even grateful one of her brothers had stepped in and put a stop to one of her bad choices in men. How many jerks had they run off over the years? Too many to count. The Knight boys were like bloodhounds with a scent for boyfriends.

"Lexi." The voice came again, and she jolted, realizing she'd been standing there staring at her hand for countless minutes while her mind tumbled over her problems. She should be paying attention to her work, considering it was a problem too. She wanted to keep this job.

"You were staring into space. Maybe I should pop next door and grab you a coffee?"

Lexi focused on the girl standing behind the counter, her boss's niece who'd been placed on the job as a — what? Threat to Lexi? She viewed it as such.

Ella May Young might be as cliché as a country girl name could get, but she was far from intimidating. She was as frightening as a sweet-faced pigeon, and while she might have been leaning against the same spot on the counter, filing her talons to perfect points the entire first hour of her shift, she appeared to be harmless to Lexi.

Actually, she made Lexi feel terrible for thinking harshly of her.

"I'm fine. I've already had coffee this morning. Just thinking about what gauge of wire to use on these blooms," she lied.

Ella bobbed her head and smiled, looking more like that cheerful pigeon Lexi likened her to, while her uncle was an owl.

She sank back into her dark musings about Matthew. What could be going on? She set down the flowers and was about to reach for the wire when a customer came in.

She looked up, features arranged into pleasantry. As Ella took the woman's name and rang up her order for her, Lexi went into the back room to retrieve the flowers from the cooler.

The minute Lexi came out of the back room carrying a huge box of flowers, Ella jumped forward to grab the other side of the box. "Oh let me help you with that, Lexi!"

Lexi couldn't help but wonder why she'd ever believed Ella to be anything but nice.

Together they carried the box to the door. "My car's just out front." The woman who'd come to collect the order for a special VIP luncheon led the way and held open the door for them.

Ella balanced the box on one hand as she juggled open the car door before the customer could reach the side.

"I could have gotten it."

"It's okay," Ella said cheerfully. "Not a problem!"

Lexi studied the girl's face. She didn't work with her very often, mostly when Ella was on college breaks. It wasn't that they didn't get along—Lexi just

51

didn't regard her as a serious worker. She was simply here at her uncle's flower shop for a seasonal restocking of her bank account.

Together, they eased the box onto the back seat of the vehicle and Ella stepped away with a sweet smile. "Thank you for your business. I hope your luncheon goes perfectly."

Feeling like the frumpy second, Lexi threw the customer an awkward wave. "Yes, thank you."

Ella walked into the shop, turning at the door to hold it open for Lexi.

Maybe she was being unkind to the girl. She didn't seem like someone set on ripping Lexi's job out from underneath her feet. Besides, she would be finishing her college education in a few months and then she'd be on to bigger and better things than her uncle's flower shop.

Inside, Lexi paused to pull a few dead petals off a flower display, expecting Ella to return to filing her nails. But she swept the file into her handbag and stowed it under the counter.

"That was a big order."

Lexi nodded. "It's a busy time of year. Lots of Mardi Gras parties and people in town to impress."

Ella smiled. "What's next on the to-do list?"

Seeing she was eager for the work for once, Lexi went to the notepad and rattled off a list. Before she'd gotten it all out, Ella had spun away to grab vases and cards to fill an order.

Seeing her bent intently over choosing the best blooms for the get-well bouquet, Lexi felt more horrible for being uncharitable about Ella coming to work with her. She might have grown up some since Christmas break. She sure seemed willing to work this time around.

"Where did you get that skirt, Lexi? It's adorable."

Shaken from her thoughts, Lexi glanced down at the pleats of her full skirt of dark purple with small gold flecks printed on the fabric. The cut was retro but the pattern modern, and she sported a waist-skimming T-shirt and a pair of flats with it for a more casual look.

"At Athena's boutique," she answered.

"Oh yes, your sister-in-law. Such a cute little store but it's just too rich for my pocketbook." She winked.

"Athena insists I take a discount or I wouldn't shop there either." She fiddled with a crate of fresh greenery.

"Your style's so unique. I feel like I should up my game if I'm working with you. After all, my uncle's shop caters to some elite clients. I need to project an image."

Lexi contemplated Ella's outfit. "Well, your skirt's a little on the short side, something you might wear to a club. And your top could be tucked in instead of knotted at the waist. If your sandals were gold, they'd be less casual and perfect for New Orleans spring."

Expecting the young woman to take offense to her critique, Lexi waited for a snotty remark, which she might have gained three months ago from the young woman.

Ella looked down at herself and then slowly began to unknot her top. She pressed the ends into her skirt and tugged the fitted garment down her sleek thighs. Glancing up, she gave Lexi a shy smile. "Is that better?"

Lexi nodded and smiled back, both surprised and relieved not to have made an enemy of the boss's niece. She had to keep working conditions easy, after all. And she loved talking clothes, shoes, accessorizing, and hair and makeup. She'd never managed to get her baby sister Tyler into a stylish ensemble for long before she'd reach for her running shorts and a tank top with some logo on the chest.

The rest of the morning was spent chattering with Ella about fashion and favorite designer lines neither of them could afford. By the time lunch rolled around, they were laughing and more at ease with each other.

When the boss came in, they were working an assembly line of bouquets and getting along like old friends. Eric smiled at them and went straight to the register. He pulled out the drawer and took it to the back room for counting.

Lexi watched him go, trying not to let Ella read the worry on her face. Hopefully one of her siblings had rubbed off their ability to hide what they were thinking about her.

Ella smiled as if putting Lexi at ease. "So, do you have anyone special in your life? A boyfriend?"

Jerking at the question, Lexi's mind leaped into the dark waters surrounding the mystery of her supposed lover. The one who'd come to the strawberry gathering hungry for anything but shortcake—and who had basically loved her and left her hanging.

Hanging for too many days now.

She pushed out a breath. "Uh, nobody really."

Just then Eric appeared in the doorway of the back room. "Lexi, can I see you for a minute?"

She froze in place, her shoes iced over to the tile floor as dread came over her. She didn't need to be told there was a discrepancy between sales and the money drawer.

She was about to be put on probation.

* * * * *

Eyes closed behind the dark shades of her sunglasses, Lexi turned her face up to the sky. Even a lounge on the deck and the sun's warmth wasn't improving her mood. Nothing could.

One more screw-up and she was out of a job.

Seems I'm out of a boyfriend too.

Her mood sank lower, and up until a few hours ago, she never would have believed she could feel worse about her life.

The back door of the house opened and closed. She opened her eyes to see a dark shape hover over her. For a second, her heart leaped with hope that it could be Matthew returning to her.

Then she realized it was Tyler.

Her sister sank to an outdoor lounge chair next to Lexi's and faced her. "What's up, Lex? *Maman* said you didn't want dinner."

"I'm not five anymore. Sometimes people don't want to eat," she snapped without sitting up or looking her direction.

Tyler didn't budge. "What's going on?"

"What the hell do you think's going on?"

"Don't get testy with me, sis. I shared a womb with you."

"And that doesn't mean you understand anything about my life."

Tyler issued a low breath that sounded full of pain. Remorse flooded Lexi, and she reached out to take Tyler's hand.

"I'm sorry, Tyleri," she used the nickname her twin hated. "I'm just in a bad mood."

"Why don't you come for a run with me? Get your mind off things."

She stared at Tyler. "What things are those?" She could not—would not—admit what had happened at work. And talking about Matthew was like bashing head-first into concrete block walls at every turn.

56

She might as well give up. If her brothers were blocking him from coming to her, then the man must not feel that strongly about her or he'd find a way.

Lexi closed her eyes and ignored her sister's request to go for a run with her. Soon, Tyler realized she wasn't going to say more and she got up and went back inside, leaving Lexi alone with a black cloud hanging over her and no hope of it blowing away.

* * * * *

Rocko was a lot of fucking things. Stubborn, willful, sometimes know-it-all—but first and foremost a Marine.

He could face down a goddamn mirror and meet the damage that had been wrought.

Pushing off the hospital bed without help was the first task at hand. No way was he going to call for a nurse just to see the pitiful expression in her eyes when she looked at the man he once was versus what he was now.

He swung his legs over the bed. He was weak— far weaker than he'd like to admit. What had happened to him in the past few weeks?

He hadn't been running full-tilt with eighty pounds of gear, that was what.

Dragging in a deep, fortifying breath, he swayed to his feet.

And nearly fell over.

He was off balance. *That happens when they take your arm.*

Feeling a mix of disgust and pure determination, he focused on his steps. One foot in front of the other all the way to the bathroom. He lurched and swayed like a monster on a horror film, one of those zombie shows maybe.

Catching onto the door frame, he hauled himself into the bathroom and faced the mirror. Eyes pinched shut, heart racing from exertion and fear.

He'd seen plenty of wounded warriors. Ran across them all the time. He'd never thought much about their dark paths leading up to the point where they could go into public after being blown up, disfigured.

Now he did.

It took guts, and Rocko might have lost some of the brass in his balls, but he could damn well face his reflection.

He moved to brace his hands on the sink and found he only had one. He tipped to the side and had to engage his abs to remain upright.

Then he opened his eyes.

Just opened them like he was waking up in the morning on an ordinary day of his life.

His stare landed on the top of his head first and the row of stitches marching over a shaved portion of his head, the source of all the itching.

Then on to his face, on healing scabs across his cheek and down to his jaw. A bigger gash there where they'd picked shrapnel out during surgery. Then to his neck.

Worse. Twisted and scarred, never the same again. But it hadn't killed him, somehow just millimeters from his jugular. Goddamn lucky, Colonel Jackson had said when he'd come to visit him.

Biting the bullet, so to speak, Rocko dropped his gaze to his shoulder.

It ended in only a sleeve of the hospital gown, a short nothing covering a ghost limb. And yeah, it was true that he still felt the missing body part. He tried to use it constantly, only to be smacked in the face with reality all over again.

Reaching behind his neck, he untied the gown and stripped it down over the healing stump that was only a few inches past his shoulder joint. Barely enough to stick a prosthetic on, but they were telling him they'd fit him for it as soon as he healed enough. Then months of rehab, learning to balance again, to move without his limb and finally to figure out how the new prosthetic worked.

They'd had some other wounded vet in here to talk to him about how he'd been sniping again within six months and Rocko would too. He hadn't listened to a bit of the bullshit coming from these guys' mouths because, fact was, he was finished.

59

A quiet knock sounded on the door just inches from the bathroom. He turned just as it opened and found himself staring at a familiar set of hazel eyes.

"Chloe." His voice came out as a harsh rasp from disuse.

Her jaw fell open and she stared at him and then dropped her gaze to his shoulder, bandaged with a mesh covering.

"What the hell are you doing here? I told the guys not to inform you of what happened." He yanked his gown back up.

His sister made a strangled noise in her throat and then threw herself at him. Wrapping her arms around him and burying her head against his good shoulder. "My God, you're a stubborn jerk, Matthew. Why wouldn't you want me to know you were hurt?"

She felt good, a link to the past and a lifeline he didn't realize he wanted or needed. He put his arm around her and held her for a long minute as she cried. His throat closed off too, but he was made of tougher stuff. No whimpering sister was going to yank a tear from these dry eyes.

He set her back from him and waved for her to go into the room. She watched him progress to the bed, doing his impression of Igor, and thank God didn't remark on it.

His foot skidded on the completely even floor. Thrown off by not having eight pounds on one side of his body, he started to go down.

Chloe cried out and reached for him, but he put down his hand—the hand that wasn't there. And smashed his face off the floor.

Pain ricocheted through his face, jarring his head that was still painful after the concussion.

"Oh my God! Matthew. Nurse!" She ran out into the hall and two nurses came rushing back in.

Fury pulsed through his system along with humiliation that ran deeper than his very bones. Goddammit, he couldn't be this man for the rest of his life, unable to even put toothpaste on his toothbrush alone let along walk across a flat surface.

He lay on his side, breathing hard as two small nurses tried to assist him into bed again while his sister got in the way.

When he'd managed to land his ass into the seat of a wheelchair, Chloe said, "Your nose is bleeding."

He waved his hand, feeling the ghost digits like they were still attached and functional. Hell, he could feel his watch attached to his wrist that wasn't there either.

Swallowing back all the angry words that threatened to spew at his sister, he allowed the nurses to assist him back to bed. He turned his head and stared at the blinds. Those chinks of light were gray today, which didn't surprise him since it matched his soul.

"I'll be right back with something to clean your nose," one of the pretty young nurses said, touching his leg. They both went out, leaving him and Chloe alone.

His sister barged into his scope of vision. He hadn't seen her in so long and he'd missed her. But he didn't want her here.

"You can go. I'm fine," he said.

She gaped at him. "I can't believe you'd even suggest such a thing. I took off work to come here and help you."

"Don't need help."

She eyed him warily, as if knowing he was close to shooting off like a cannon. "Okay, so I'm here for moral support. Everybody needs it, and from what your friends tell me, you won't accept any help. They said you've been cleared to start rehab but you just haven't done it. You realize you can't stay in this bed forever, Matthew."

"I fucking know it!" His voice came out as a bellow, and Chloe winced.

"Go on and get mad. I can deal with your moods. I'm still not leaving. I'm here to help you for as long as you need me."

"You have a life. You can't just drop everything for me," he muttered.

"Andrew's holding down the fort. That's what husbands do when it comes to family. He's capable of taking care of Riley and he's supportive of me coming here. My boss too. I had a month of vacation saved up."

"You should go to Aruba instead."

She burst out laughing. "I'd rather, you ass. If you'd show me that you're on the path to recovery, then I could still take that week at the end of the month. Now let's make a plan and get you to a better place so I can soak up the sun, okay?"

He felt like a chastised toddler and liked it even less than falling flat on his face. He didn't have an opportunity to respond to Chloe's speech, though, because the head nurse came in to examine his nose while another cleaned away the blood.

He sniffed. "It's not broken."

"It could be cracked," the nurse said.

"I've had a broken nose before and it's not broken."

"All right. Well, I'll let you have your visit and then we need to start talking about you getting out of bed without help when you need to be taught the skills first." The nurse exchanged a look with his sister, and he wished to hell he could get up and leave this place.

After the nurses bustled out of the room, his sister sank to the edge of his bed. They stared at each other. She reached for his hand, and he let her have it, the fight gone for the moment.

"I'm here for you, Matthew. We're family. We've always stuck together."

He didn't say anything.

"After Mom left, you took care of me. Always. It's my turn to return the favor." She searched his face, and he saw the girl he'd grown up protecting and helping through her awkward teen years when their dad was worthless with that sort of thing. He'd been the one to go out and buy her supplies for her first period.

"Okay, so that's settled," she said brusquely. "You'll begin rehab as soon as it can be arranged. I'll stay with you. And we'll have lots of opportunity to talk about things."

He eyed her. "What things?"

"How about we start with that woman you're in love with? I want to hear all about Lexi first, and why you won't tell her what happened to you."

* * * * *

Lexi tucked her hair over her shoulder and adjusted her necklace. The woman looking back at her in the mirror had once been bright-eyed with happiness but not anymore. Each day she got ready for work, she found herself anxiety-ridden from walking on eggshells. Throw in a huge dollop of rejection from Matthew and she was pretty damn miserable.

A low voice came from downstairs, and she cocked her head, listening harder.

When she opened to door to hear even better, her heart started pounding.

Dylan was here.

If she could corner her brother, she might be able to drag some information from him.

Taking off down the stairs, she landed in the living room in front of him and her father. Their heads were bent together and they spoke in low voices, but she'd caught her name.

"What's this about me?" She barged into the middle of the pair.

They straightened away from each other and Dylan did that thing with his jaw that told her he was getting ready to tell a lie.

She grabbed him by the shoulders and glared up at him. Of all her brothers, he was the most levelheaded when it came to her boyfriends.

"Don't you even think of lying to me, Dylan Knight. Every one of you is avoiding me, and I want to know why." She curled her fingers into his shoulders hard. "Now."

He shot a look at their father for help, and she shifted to stand between them.

"Oh no, he can't save you. Dylan. The truth." She emphasized each word with a widening of her eyes.

Dylan reached up, peeled her hands off his shoulders and gently clasped both her hands. "Lex, we're all just busy."

"Where's Rocko?"

"He's just tied up, is all."

She tore her hands away and went for his neck. He laughed and dodged her grip. Backing up, he executed an evasion tactic but she was having none of it. Behind them, their father chuckled.

She stalked Dylan into a corner. Figuring she wasn't going to bully him into giving her the answers she wanted, she switched to puppy dog eyes.

He dropped his head back and stared at the ceiling. "Don't do that to me, Lexi. Dammit, you know I can't stand when you give me that look."

She grabbed him by the nape and yanked his head down to meet her pleading stare.

"She's got you now, son," their father said.

"*Papa*. Help," he said.

"You're on your own. You know my feelings on the matter."

She let go of her brother and whirled to face her *papa*. "Then there *is* a matter? Tell me what's going on!"

While she made demands of her father, the front door slammed shut. She ran to the door, a growl of despair and frustration on her lips. She yanked open the door and yelled at her rotten brother's retreating back. "You better believe I'll remember this! Wait till your wife wants a pretty baby shower and you don't know how to go about it!" She slammed the door shut again and folded her arms.

Dammit, she'd been wasting time laboring under the belief that Matthew had actually walked away from everything they'd shared that day. When really it *was* her conniving brothers the whole time.

She met her father's gaze and opened her mouth.

"I'm Switzerland."

"Dammit," she said under her breath. She was just going to have to figure out another method to get what she wanted. Ben, Sean and Dylan were no-gos. Her sisters-in-law as well, and her father was Switzerland.

Pushing out a heavy sigh, she grabbed her handbag and keys and walked out of the house.

Since none of her family was talking, she had to resort to other measures. She drove straight to Colonel Jackson's house. She'd spent a lot of time talking to him over the months since her brother had been married to the colonel's only daughter. She liked the man, despite his gruff exterior and eagle eyes that missed nothing.

Hopefully that last trait worked in her favor today. If anyone knew what was going on with Matthew, it was Jackson.

The road to the colonel's beautiful historical home was lush with spring vegetation and if Lexi was in a different frame of mind, she'd enjoy every minute of it. She was a simple girl and found contentment in the small things in life. Which was why she was so unhappy right now. Nothing was simple, easy or remotely peaceful.

When she pulled into the long driveway leading to the big house, she chewed her bottom lip. Then cursed as she rounded a bend in the drive and spotted Ben's car.

Just what I need — more guard dogs. Well, she'd find a way to get her interfering brother out of the way.

When she got out of the car, she drew in a deep breath of the flowers lining the sidewalk. Sweet and fragrant, but they did nothing to calm her nerves.

She was getting answers — now.

She knocked on the door and damn if her brother didn't open it.

"What the fuck?" he said.

She pushed past him without a word. "I'm here to find out what happened to Rocko, and you can't stop me." She raised her voice, and it echoed through the high ceilings. "Colonel Jackson? Colonel?"

"Jesus, Lexi, get a hold of yourself. You can't just come in here making demands."

She whipped around to settle a glare on Ben that resulted in a wince from him. Any other time, she'd smirk about hitting where she aimed, but she was too upset right now.

The colonel appeared carrying Ben and Dahlia's beautiful little girl on his arm, a woman behind him. Ah, the one the guys talked about him going all midlife crisis for, buying a Harley Davidson and takin' beach vacations with. She looked normal enough to Lexi and gave her a smile.

Lexi gave one back and then turned to the one man she was setting her faith in. "Can I speak to you alone?"

"Not without me," Ben said.

"Of course, I have plenty of time for you, Lexi." He handed off the baby to the woman and led the way to his office. The dark paneling that was original to the house gleamed with polish, and two windows were carved between a massive wall of bookcases.

"Close the door," Jackson said.

Ben did so and Lexi faced the man. "I'm here to find out what happened to Rocko. Nobody will give me a straight answer, and I can't find him. If he's dead..." Her worst fear, and one she hadn't spoken or even allowed herself to think until now. Her voice broke and she came to a halt, unable to say more around the emotion choking her.

Ben pushed out a sigh and Jackson looked from her to her brother. "Why the hell hasn't this girl been informed."

Her knees buckled and she sat down hard on a leather chair. Quaking inside like a leaf in a hurricane, barely clinging to a branch of reality.

Matthew was dead.

Someone had finally verified it.

"He's not dead," Jackson said with a matter-of-factness that had her gulping against tears.

"He's... not?"

"Jesus, she's so pale. Ben, get her a drink. Brandy."

She hated brandy but right about now, she'd take anything that might fortify her through this ordeal.

Ben went to the side of the room and removed the stopper from a bottle of brandy and then poured three drinks. Oh boy. Clearly they'd all need one for this.

She got to her feet, wobbling slightly from the previous shock.

"Please sit down, Lexi," Jackson urged.

She did and then accepted the drink from Ben. She wrapped her hands around the glass and took a sip, noting how unsteady her hands were. "Where is he?" she managed in a hoarse whisper.

"He's alive," Jackson reiterated.

Alive. Nothing more.

"What happened?" she asked Ben.

"He stepped into range of some explosive."

"Range?"

"Yes."

"Meaning he was blown up." Her voice came out flat.

"I can't believe you boys didn't tell Rocko's girlfriend what happened to him."

Shocked, she stared at Jackson. Even he knew she was his girlfriend.

Was she his girlfriend then?

Gathering her wits, she said, "But he's okay."

Ben and Jackson exchanged a look, and then Ben set down his drink and came to crouch in front of Lexi. "Look, he didn't want us to tell you—"

She'd smack his handsome face if it wasn't such a show of disrespect to the colonel's hospitality. Ben was his guest, after all.

So she threw her drink in his face.

The brandy washed down over his skin to wet his shirt collar.

"You tell me right now. Everything."

Jackson passed Ben a bar towel, and he dried himself without looking back over his shoulder at his father-in-law and superior.

"There was an explosion. We got him lifted out and he's had some surgeries."

Oh God. He was disfigured. Not that she cared. He'd always be the man she loved.

"But he's alive," she said again.

"Yes. He doesn't want to see you."

Nothing could have run a blade through her like those words. Jaw dropped, she gasped. After a heartbeat, she regained her stamina. She *was* a Knight, after all.

"Like hell he won't see me."

"Lexi, give him some time. We're trying to bring him around, get him to talk to you at least on the phone—"

"That's ridiculous. If he loves me like he told me he does, then he'll see me. Tell me where he is." She got to her feet and directed the question at Jackson.

"He's in a rehab unit now."

"Okay, give me the name and I'll go there now."

"Lexi." Ben's voice was strange enough to make her turn.

When she looked into his eyes, she saw the pain he'd been bearing for his friend, trying to hide all this time.

"Let me speak to him before I tell you where he is," Jackson said.

"I don't understand what can be so terrible that he refuses to see me. I don't care if half his face is missing."

They exchanged a look.

"Oh God. All his face is missing?" She shook herself. "I don't care. I love him. I'll be there for him."

"No, Lexi, his face is all right," Ben said.

"But you won't tell me how to find him."

"Not yet," Jackson said slowly. "I'll go to him later today and settle things." He came forward to rest a hand on her shoulder. The gesture made her melt under the duress and she broke down completely.

Jackson stepped back, unsure how to handle a crying female, and Ben stepped up to take her in his arms. The big, comforting chest of her brother wasn't touching this problem, though. She wasn't crying over some little heartbreak—the man she loved and wanted to spend the rest of her life with had been lying in a hospital injured for weeks, and she hadn't been there for him. Because he didn't want her there.

Drawing free of her brother's hold, she went back through the house and out the front door. Still weeping, she got behind the wheel and drove away, not even seeing the beauty of the countryside now. Seeing nothing but her man, who had somehow gotten her brothers to agree to keep her away.

He was hurt bad enough to be in rehab. All that mattered right now was that she could go to him and help him.

Well, at least she'd gotten to the bottom of the mystery, even if it'd made her impossibly late for her shift at the flower shop and she'd just put her job on the line more than ever.

None of that mattered, though. A job was a job. But love was everything.

Chapter Five

Rocko settled onto the padded tabletop and waited to be given the same old exercises from the physical therapist. Ten reps of this, ten of that. None of them challenging.

None would help him get back to his former physical ability, even with this new prosthetic he wore fitted over his stump.

It wasn't that he was against trying to make the most of the new arm, but he knew it would never be the same. If he was lucky, he'd be an everyday Joe, able to pull up his own pants and make coffee. But he wanted so much more.

"Your sister didn't come along today?" Jory asked. The physical therapist was ex-military as well and refused daily to take even an ounce of Rocko's shit. It amused and infuriated him at the same time.

"Her husband and son came to town and they're taking some time together."

"That's nice. So," Jory positioned herself in front of Rocko, "you ready to work for me today?"

"I would if you'd actually give me some work."

She arched a brow. "Is that the challenge I've been waiting for?"

He snorted. "Doubt it."

"Why don't we see? On your feet."

He stood and Jory pointed to the gym mat on the floor. "I assume you're like every other Marine I've ever crossed paths with and you think you're the king of the one-armed pushup."

He stared at her. "You want me to do pushups? With this thing?" He still had little control over the prosthetic and he flapped it at her.

"I want you to get your stamina up again and give me the one-armed pushups. The prosthetic will serve as a way to steady yourself to start. Now drop and give me five."

He scoffed. "Five. Do you think I'm a kindergartener?"

She braced her legs wide. "We'll see, won't we?"

He eased himself onto the mat. In the past, he'd bent one arm behind his back, but it was impossible to do that with the prosthetic, at least for the time being. When it hung there against the mat, he issued a curse.

"C'mon, Marine. Give it your all."

He grunted and dipped. Once, twice. By the fourth pushup, he was tipping precariously to the side but managed the fifth before he collapsed. "Dammit!"

Applause filled the room. Too loud to be only one person. He glared up, thinking to see his sister there but was faced with Ben.

He jackknifed up into a sitting position and concentrated hard on getting his new arm to do his bidding. Sean walked in followed by Dylan.

"Jesus, what is this? A Knight reunion?" he muttered.

Chaz entered next, and he figured the line would end there but then Tyler and Bo crowded into the room.

He scrambled to his feet, heart drumming. If Lexi was next, so help him, he was never going to forgive these people for not keeping his secret. He stared at the door, burning with fear. Burning with excitement.

"She's not here. But you're damn lucky she didn't follow us," Tyler said, folding her arms and staring down Rocko.

"Knowing our sister, she probably did."

Jory made a noise, and Rocko said, "This is Jory." He waved toward her. Everyone gaped at him. "What the fuck's your problem?"

"You used your arm," Sean said.

"And? Am I supposed to be proud of a little flick of a chunk of titanium?"

"Actually, it's carbon fiber, but I'll just take my leave." Jory edged around the wall of Knight Ops flesh, leaving him to deal with the crew.

He looked around at the group. "What are you doing here? You can't need me for some mission. I'm sidelined, remember?"

Ben gave a shake of his head. "We're here because of Lexi."

His chest seized, a tightening that he couldn't breathe around. "What about her? It's over."

"Like hell," Dylan drawled.

"What's holding you back?" Ben asked.

"What's...? Are you fucking kidding me? It takes me three minutes to get my dick out of my pants so I can take a piss. What am I supposed to do with your sister? Besides, when did you decide that I should have anything to do with Lexi? Two months ago, you would have cut off my balls and shoved them down my throat for even looking her direction."

Hawk was chuckling, and Tyler punched him in the upper arm.

"So you're saying we've been holding you back," Ben said.

This was freakin' crazy. Never had he imagined himself in this situation, with Lexi's family who'd once warned him off her to be standing in front of him telling him he needed to see her.

"Yeah, that's what I'm saying," Rocko said. "Or *was* saying. You can't tell me that if I'd told you how I felt about your sister, you would have gone along with it. Welcomed me into the family."

"Man, if we've accepted Hawk's dumb ass into the family, we'd accept you too," Sean said.

"Thanks, bro. Love you too." Hawk thumped his chest with a fist and Sean did the same in return.

He walked to the other side of the room and grabbed a bottle of water. Then on second thought, remembering what Jory would say, he set it back down and reached for it with his prosthetic.

The room seemed to go silent as they all watched his attempt. He focused on closing the fingers around the center of the plastic bottle. He lifted and moved it in front of him to twist off the cap with the other hand.

His grip was too light and he twisted it right out of his hand. The water fell with a splash. "Goddammit!" Rocko swiped it off the floor with his good hand and whipped it against the wall, where the plastic cracked and water flooded out.

He whirled on the group. "You're wasting your time! I can't have her! I'm half a fucking man!"

Tyler stepped up. "You're far from that, Rocko."

"Yeah, you're going to face these challenges but in another few months, this will be normal to you. There won't be anything you can't do," Chaz added.

Rocko met Chaz's stare. They'd faced so much together. All of them had. This was one more obstacle.

Or it was the end of the line.

He twisted away from them. "What if it was you, huh? That you couldn't hold your wives, your kids?"

"You've still got one good arm to do those things, and this one will be in your control in no time," Dylan said.

"Look, she's hurting too, man." Ben's words had him turning. He saw the truth on his buddy's face and the thought of him being the cause of Lexi's pain slayed him.

"And she's pissed," Tyler said.

"Pissed doesn't begin to describe it. She's fucking nuclear, man. She went to Jackson," Ben said.

"Jesus." The thought of his little Lexi showing up on Jackson's doorstep and making demands for information about his whereabouts had his chest welling with emotion.

"She won't leave us alone. She wants to know where you're at."

"She knows something happened?" His voice came out as a harsh whisper.

Tyler nodded. "She knows you've been injured but she doesn't know where you are. If she did, she'd be standing here with her hands on her hips telling you off for herself. You can't keep her away forever, Rocko."

Looking into Tyler's eyes reminded him so much of what he should be fighting for. He spun away and pinched the bridge of his nose with his good hand. "I'll think on it. That's all I can offer right now."

Ben came forward and squeezed his shoulder. "We'll get out of your way. Let you get back to your half-assed pushups. You can do better."

"Asshole." Rocko would have laughed if he didn't feel like crying his eyes out like a toddler.

The Knight family all left him alone with his thoughts and a truckload of pain and confusion.

Lexi deserved to know what was happening and when she saw what he'd become, then she'd be able to make the right choice.

Then she'd be able to walk away from him.

* * * * *

When Chloe poked her head around the door of Rocko's room, he groaned and rolled his eyes. A grin jumped across her features, and she came inside looking like he'd just made her day.

"I see you're in one of your normal moods." Her cheeks were rosy and her eyes glimmered.

"That's a good thing?" he grumbled.

"It is since it's the most 'you' thing I've seen since coming here." She dropped into the seat next to his bed. "I heard your team was here."

He rolled his eyes again. "I bet that was the talk of the place." Five huge guys and a tough Marine woman storming into the rehab facility didn't go unnoticed.

She nodded and folded her hands over her stomach, leaning back in the chair. "You betcha. Now tell me what happened that put you into a better mood."

He arched a brow. "Again, you think I'm in a better mood?" He wasn't—not by far. The conclusion

80

he'd come to left him aching more than he did for his own goddamn arm.

"Okay," she said after a few silent moments, "if you won't tell me that, then at least fill me in on your training session today. I heard good things."

"If you already know what happened, then why bother askin'?" He got out of bed and walked to the window. Looking out over a parking lot at the overhead lamps glowing dimly over the shadowy world. What he wouldn't give for a good whiff of salty Gulf air right now.

Or bayou.

Visions jumped into his head of times spent with the Knight family at their cabin. Being invited was always a treat and one he luxuriated in. Having the time to just kick back, drink some beers and eat a good homecooked meal...

And to watch Lexi.

The woman made every occasion into something special. Hell, she made cheap box wine seem chic. And she could toss on some disreputable T-shirt from one of her larger male relations and appear to have just stepped off the pages of some glamour magazine.

But those weren't even the things that drew Rocko to her.

She had the sweetest disposition of any woman he'd ever met. She loved showering her loved ones with small personal touches like a flower left on a pillowcase. Or frying their bacon to the perfect crispness.

On the other hand, maybe it was her toughness that got Rocko's blood heating. She took no bullshit off her brothers and he'd seen her untangle herself from a wrestling hold and then end up on top of the pile, forcing her brothers to beg for mercy.

A smile came to his lips, just a touch of one. But it was the first he'd experienced since that fateful day when he'd been injured.

No, irreparably damaged.

"Matthew." His sister's voice rang out with that wheedling tone she used to drive him crazy with as a kid. It meant she wanted him to tell her something, and she used it on everything from finding out what her birthday present was to who he secretly had a crush on.

He turned from the window.

"Tell me about Lexi."

He stared at her for a long minute. "There's nothing to say. It's over before it started."

"That's not what your expression says."

He slashed the air with his hand, and after the fact realized he'd used the prosthetic. More and more he was growing accustomed to it—it was becoming an extension of him. Though it still felt foreign as hell.

His movement wasn't lost on his sister either. Her smile was back in place, broader than before.

Clearly, he was going to have to do something to shut her up before she started gushing about his improvement.

"Lexi's always been off-limits."

"Seems odd, considering her family is urging you to see her."

"How the hell do you know this? Did you get the nurses to eavesdrop on us?"

She waved a hand too. "I just know. You're not the only Rock who can keep secrets. So if they want you to see Lexi, that old excuse for not seeing her is null and void, right?"

He chewed the inside of his cheek. "It's more complex than that."

"Then explain it to me."

He needed to move. He started to pace, back and forth in front of the windows with the terrible view, his jumbled thoughts coming to some kind of order so he could put it into words for Chloe.

He stopped moving and met his sister's gaze. "She deserves better."

"Better than a man who's got a position on one of the most elite special ops team in the world?"

"Did have."

She shook her head. "What I hear is that the minute you've got your reflexes up and your group is consistent on the target, you're back. So that reason doesn't fly with me. Because if you can perform in the Knight Ops team, you can do anything, brother."

He pushed out a low growl. "You don't understand."

"Then explain it to me. Because no, I don't see why hiding from the woman you love—who is in love with you—is best for either of you."

He rubbed his fingers over his head. "You can't understand because it's not your arm. Not your life. Chloe, it's hard enough for me to go on and relearn absolutely everything let alone figure out how to be a lover to a woman like Lexi."

She gazed at him for a long heartbeat. "She's just a woman, Matthew. She isn't a goddess or some royal princess. She wants your love and—"

He cut her off. "I'm not in the mood, Chloe. If you're here to dig at me about my choices then you're wasting your time."

Compressing her lips, she gave a nod and then slowly stood. Too late he realized she was about to go. "You're right. I'll let you think on things. I'll come back tomorrow."

"I won't see things any differently," he murmured.

She came up to rest a hand on his shoulder. "Think about this, Matthew. Your arguments only benefit yourself. Because I didn't hear anything in what you said that was for Lexi."

With that, she walked out. When he looked out at the ugly, gray parking lot again, he sank deeper into depression. Yeah, he was a lot of things—sniper, master of war, prankster, asshole.

But never in his life had he been selfish.

He walked out of the room and headed to the gym. If he couldn't think straight, the least he could do was run to clear his head. If nothing else, he could still use his legs.

Yeah, he could run out of this place straight to Lexi.

* * * * *

When Lexi walked into the flower shop and set down her purse, she turned to find Ella leaning against the counter. She didn't have a nail file in hand but was just staring at her.

"Uh, hi," Lexi said.

She gave a smile that was only a sad tightening of her lips before she looked away.

Crap. What was happening here? Always one to face things head-on, she turned to her coworker.

"Okay, what's going on?" she asked.

Ella let her gaze slide away. "Nothing…"

"Is your uncle here?"

She bit down on her pink lower lip and shook her head. "He'll be here this afternoon, but I'm not supposed to tell you."

Fantastic. He'd probably found another error on her part, though she'd double-checked each and every sum twice.

Ella gave her a compassionate look. Lexi balled her fist at her side. If that had been one of her family members looking at her this way, they'd be swallowing their teeth right now. But she couldn't physically attack Ella and walk away without assault charges.

Her mind rolled over what was about to happen and what she could do to control any of it.

For the past two weeks, she'd been thinking hard about her situation. She couldn't go to her brothers or sister—they'd all make her feel lesser with their pity. The last thing she needed.

She could talk to her parents but she'd always felt they personally carried the weight of her disability as their own doing, even though neither had any control over her lack of oxygen at birth. Besides, Tyler had come out after her and been totally fine.

No, she had to do this on her own, and there was only one person she knew who could help. Someone good with numbers and who wouldn't look down on her.

Someone who owed her a favor because she might have gotten him a great rate on the flowers for his wedding.

She edged past Ella and went into the back room. There she hurriedly opened the file drawer and yanked out two files she knew contained the last register printouts. Throwing a look over her shoulder, she stuffed both into her big purse and then went out front. Luckily, Ella was waiting on a customer and couldn't say anything about Lexi leaving.

If she was going to be fired, what would it matter if she missed a few hours of her shift? Walking up the sidewalk toward the coffeeshop, she dialed her friend's number and brought her cell to her ear.

"Brett."

"If it isn't Miss Knight." His Southern drawl hit her ear like molasses.

"It's about lunchtime for you, isn't it? What do you say about meeting me at the coffeeshop near me and I'll buy you a sandwich."

"One of those ones on the homemade bagels?"

"The very one."

"You're on. And I'll bring my calculator, shall I?"

"Yes." Relief sang through her veins that he knew exactly what her reason was for calling. After all these years, her old math tutor was still there for her.

She ended the call just as she breezed through the door of the coffeeshop. The fragrant aroma of fresh brew hit her senses, along with a hint of the yeasty bagels Brett was anticipating. She snagged a corner booth and tucked her purse close to her side. Not that anybody knew what she was hiding inside it. If her boss found out, she'd be in deep shit, but what did a little risk matter when she was already operating on borrowed time?

She was as good as fired anyway. The only thing she had left was her dignity and her good name, and she planned to walk away with both.

A waitress came for her order, and she took the liberty of ordering for Brett too—fresh pot of coffee, ice waters, turkey and ham sandwiches on fresh everything bagels with lettuce and their special homemade mayo.

"Oh and a dish of pickles," she added before the waitress walked away.

She turned with a grin. "You got it."

Lexi tapped her feet under the table and wiped her sweaty palms against her skirt. By the time Brett walked in, her skirt was wrinkled when she stood to greet him.

He kissed her on the cheek and embraced her warmly.

"How are you?" she asked. "You look wonderful. Married life agrees with you."

He gave her a crooked smile. "That's odd to hear, since I'm getting a divorce."

Her jaw dropped. "I'm so sorry."

He slid into the padded booth seat and she did the same. They faced each other across the table. After a moment, she said, "What happened?"

"Clearly she wasn't as into it as I was. I should have known when I was more excited about planning the wedding than she was."

Lexi took his hands across the table and squeezed them. "Then she wasn't deserving of you, and when you're ready, the right person will be standing in front of you."

He gave a doleful smile. "We'll see how I feel down the road. Right now, I'm pretty raw. But that's all about me for now. You need help."

She nodded and started to clue him in on the entire debacle at the flower shop. As she drew the two files from her bag, their food arrived. They put aside the work in trade for the delicious bagel sandwiches and piping hot coffee.

When she couldn't eat another bite, she slid her plate away and reached for the files.

"What do we have? Printouts?" he asked.

"Yes." He drew the file toward him, and she stopped him with a hand on his. They looked at each other. "Brett, I can't thank you enough. I've been really..." She trailed off, her throat closing on emotion.

"I know. You've always been much harder on yourself for your shortcomings than anybody else ever was."

"I don't like people looking down on me."

"We've discussed this how many times now? Nobody looks down on you, Lexi. They might want to help, but they aren't doing it because they pity you. Now." He smiled at her and released her hands so he could take out his calculator and pen.

She watched him work for a minute, thinking how studious he always appeared with his wire-rimmed glasses and the way that lock of hair fell over his forehead. Then she looked up toward the front of the restaurant.

Her breath hitched. She did a double-take.

There in the doorway stood a huge man, a warrior.

A man whose eyes were burning as he stared at her.

At that moment, Brett reached for the file and their hands brushed.

The man in the door twisted away.

She shot to her feet. "Matthew!" She surged out of the booth and nearly face-planted. She stumbled to gain her footing and ran after him.

As she shoved outside, she was aware that everyone in the coffeeshop thought her insane, and she couldn't care less. She looked right and left, spotting the familiar broad back but...

"Matthew!"

She ran after him, and he stopped in his tracks but didn't turn. As she reached for his arm, he jerked and she realized what was different.

His arm was shaped different, the shoulder narrower.

90

She jumped in front of him and threw up her hands to trap him, though he could pick her up and set her aside like a pesky flea. "Matthew, what are you doing here? Oh my God, I'm so glad to see you." The tears that had been just beneath the surface for so many weeks since she'd last seen him erupted, spilled over. They rolled down her cheeks as she stared up at the man she loved and the man who was so clearly changed.

Not just the scar slicing across his scalp or the puckered bit at the corner of one beautiful eye. But the look in those eyes was colder, more detached.

Her anger rose up.

"Where the hell have you been? Why haven't you come to me before now? I know you were in the hospital, that something happened." She broke off, looking over his arm and realizing with a shock that it was a fake, a biomechanical arm.

And the scars she was seeing went far deeper than she could ever have guessed.

Her tears flowed faster as he watched her come to this realization.

"Matthew—"

He stood cold and stiff, far from the man she knew.

"Go back to your guy." His voice was broken glass under a boot heel.

She blinked. "My... No, that's not my guy."

91

"Goddammit, I shouldn't have come." He took off walking, weaving in and out of pedestrians so she had to run to keep up and bashed right into a woman, nearly knocking her to the cement.

"Stop, Matthew! You came all the way here to see me. Now dammit, stop and face me like a man!"

She balled her fists and watched him come to a stop. People around them stared.

Then he whipped around, grabbed her by the elbow and marched her around the corner. Pressing her against a building, he glared down at her.

Her insides melted as she realized her big, hunky warrior was really here, and whether or not he was changed didn't matter. Because she was still head over freakin' high heels in love with him.

"Dammit, Lexi, go back to the coffeeshop and we'll forget that we ever saw each other."

Her heart shattered but its jagged edges cut through her, and everyone knew that any Knight who got hurt got mad.

"You're stupider than I thought. How could you hide this from me, then say that night meant nothing to us? I've spent weeks angry and aching for you, confused and hurt. Then I found out you were in the hospital but refused to allow my siblings to tell me where. Did you think you were protecting me? Because all you did was hurt me, Rocko."

"And I've battled too—don't think for a moment I haven't." His words cut across her, harsh and filled with restrained fury. "I agonized, spent weeks angry and aching for you. Was confused and hurt. You know why? Because of this." He thrust his prosthetic hand beneath her nose.

She closed her eyes.

"See? You can't even look at me now. I spent the first weeks wishing I would've died and the rest working round the clock to grip better and make the most of this thing. I dreamed of you every fucking night, Lexi, and woke in such need…" He broke off, struggling. "Then I go to the flower shop and am told you walked out. Which isn't like you. But I know right where you'll be and sure enough, I walk into that place and find you with that, that—"

"Accountant! My old tutor, Matthew."

He jerked away from her. "Go back to your accountant. Let him tutor you."

She blinked at the man's retreating back.

It took her three heartbeats to realize he was walking away from her. Probably for good.

"Matthew!" Her voice came out as a wail but he kept walking.

Oh hell no. She wasn't standing for this sort of behavior.

She took off after him. As her heels pounded the sidewalk, he threw a look over his shoulder. "Matthew Rock, you stop right there."

"Lexi, don't make me tell you again."

She grabbed him by the shoulder and yanked him around. He felt odd beneath her touch, but she forced herself not to let it show on her features.

"You've been through some shit, that's true. But you came here to find me. Did you just want to say hello and then walk away?"

He stopped and looked at her. "Look, I shouldn't have come. I made a mistake."

"The only mistake you've made is believing that I am having a romantic lunch with my accountant and tutor. Now stop being dumb."

His Adam's apple bobbed up and down his throat, which also bore a puckered scar, newly healed and still red. "Lexi, you deserve so much better than me."

She opened her mouth to stop him, but he interrupted.

"You deserve someone who can hold you with both arms. What happened between us was a mistake and it's over."

She sucked in a sharp breath, stunned. He might as well have slapped her across the face. Pain rocketed to her every nerve ending as she watched him in shock as he walked away.

Well, one good thing had come out of this. At least now she knew what had happened to him. Along with losing his arm, it seemed Matthew had lost his damn mind.

* * * * *

He'd never enjoyed the long runs in basic, and he sure as hell didn't care for it in his spare time, since he found himself sprinting while laden with heavy gear. Yet the past couple weeks, he'd made peace with the activity. He found that moving his arms and legs in sync gave him a new feeling of freedom that he craved right now.

As he pounded the streets to get away from Lexi, his mind whirled with images of her sitting across from that guy, knowing she'd be so much better off — so much happier — with anyone but himself.

Rocko didn't want to think about the pain echoing in her voice when she'd called after him or the way her hazel eyes had swam with tears when he'd said the harsh words ending it once and for all.

A mistake. It's over.

Yes, it was. Though he'd cherish that one time when his self-control had slipped and he'd bore her back on her floral-patterned bed and shared long kisses, soft words and the most mind-blowing orgasm of his goddamn life.

It came down to one thing with Lexi — he wanted her to be happy. Letting go was the only way. Until he'd seen her with his own two eyes, he'd held a thread of hope, but now he saw that was stupidity.

He ran through the streets until his thighs began to burn, but he pushed himself on. Then, suddenly noticing his surroundings, he came to a dead stop.

Somehow, his legs had carried him right back to where he'd started. He stood before the coffeeshop, but it had been too long and no way was Lexi still inside.

Even knowing he wouldn't see her, he glanced into the window.

His heart gave a hard pulse so painful that he gasped for air.

She was seated in the same booth, alone. A single cup of coffee in front of her, her head bowed and her hands in her lap.

Torn, he continued to stand there.

"Excuse me, are you going in?" someone asked.

He shifted to the side to let the person pass.

When the door opened, a waft of coffee came out, and he swore he scented her light perfume as well. The same scent that had been all over those slinky red panties.

Over her inner thighs.

At the crux of her when he'd sunk his tongue into her wet folds.

A shudder ran through him and he felt the door hit his palm. He stepped over the threshold, gaze locked on the one person who'd made his life worth fighting for.

The noise of the coffeeshop filled his ears but he barely registered anything but the pounding of his own heartbeat in his ears.

As he looked on, she pulled several napkins from the dispenser on the table and brought the wad to her eyes.

She was crying.

He moved through the space, across black and white tiled floor and past a wall of bagels in baskets. As he neared the booth, he caught the faint hiccup of her tears.

"Lexi."

She jerked her head up to look at him, eyes red and swollen.

He couldn't take it. His heart knew what it wanted, and it wanted to live—for Lexi. With Lexi.

He grabbed her and hauled her out of the booth and into his arms. She came easily, all soft curves and silky dark hair.

For the first time, he moved his prosthetic arm to put it around her, hauling her against his chest and cupping her face with his hand a split second before he kissed her.

Claimed her was more like it.

She made a noise of want in the back of her throat, and he swept his tongue through her mouth, tasting salty tears and coffee and pure woman.

"Oh God," she burst out, wrapping her arms around his shoulders.

He slanted his mouth over hers, garnering a moan from her and answering with a growl of his own. Someone whistled and another person muttered something about getting a room.

He broke free, breathing hard as he stared down at her.

"Maybe you're not as *cooyon* as I thought," she said.

He'd laugh at her using her Cajun to refer to him as stupid but he deserved it.

"We need to talk," he grated out.

"We need more kissin'."

He let his gaze travel over her tear-stained cheeks, feeling like the lowest scum for putting them there. "Where can we go?"

She blinked up at him as if realizing something for the first time. "Oh God. I never went back to work. I've been so distracted, stuck in my own world."

He smoothed his hand over her shining hair. "You need to finish your shift and I'll come for you after?"

"I…" She faltered and bit off whatever she'd been about to say. "I have to take something back. They'll know it's missing."

Staring at her in confusion, he watched her gather her bag and drape the strap over her shoulder. She placed some bills on the table for her coffee and a tip and dragged in a deep breath.

"I don't know what to think about any of this, Matthew."

"To be honest, I don't either. But I'm here right now, where I want to be."

She nodded and dropped her gaze to his arm. In a short-sleeve shirt, it was unmistakably a battle scar.

They walked out of the coffeeshop. He'd come to see if he could find a future with the woman who took up so much real estate in his heart, only to run away. If he was honest, it was his own fears he'd been running from. But now that he had her hand firmly in his, he wasn't going to let go at least until she told him she was ready to move on.

After they reached the flower shop, she didn't meet his gaze. "I'll just... go in. Can I call you in a few hours?"

He could see the inside was busy and another girl was waiting the counter and trying to speak on the telephone while others waited for her assistance.

He felt bad he'd kept Lexi from the work she loved.

"Call me. I'll be waiting." He leaned in and brushed his lips between her brows. He felt them pucker for a moment and then she relaxed against him. When she drew away and went inside, he watched her go.

The girl behind the counter looked up and glared at her, and Lexi breezed into the back room. A second later, she returned without her bag. Then she immediately began helping customers.

He stood on the sidewalk a moment longer, watching her. Her shoulders were tense. She didn't smile.

Something was stressing her out, and that something was most likely him.

What did he think? That he could just lock her out of his life and then drag her back in on his whim? No wonder she didn't look happy.

Feeling low at what he'd done, he started walking the streets of New Orleans, thinking of ways to make it up to the woman he loved.

Chapter Six

"You didn't come back all day!" Ella rounded on her the minute the shop was empty.

"I know. I'm sorry." There was nothing else to say.

"Well, where were you? My uncle was looking for you."

Her stomach sank to her knees and kept on going. "What did he want me for?"

Ella arched a brow. "You're on probation, Lexi. I'm sure you know that failing to show up for your shift caused him some distress."

She pressed her lips together tight and carried the water jug to the sink. As she filled it from the faucet, she played over what had happened to her and what might happen yet.

She'd returned to the coffeeshop, heartbroken and weeping, to learn that Brett had found several discrepancies himself and unfortunately, they were all on her register time.

Yes, she'd made the mistakes. But in the course of the day, did it really matter? Rocko had returned to her. And lost an arm. Who knew what else the poor man had endured alone, though the ass should have called her.

First he'd shown up just to tell her it was all a mistake? But then returned to her and kissed her like a man who had been waiting to do nothing else in his entire life.

She had whiplash and no wonder.

But regardless of her personal life and what happened with Matthew, she still had big problems to deal with here at work.

Brett had been kind, seeing her distress, and offered to meet up another day when things were easier for her. He'd taken the printouts next door to photocopy so he could study the bookkeeping more in depth, and then promised to be in touch.

She started filling the water containers holding fresh-cut blooms while Ella watched.

"So you're staying to work the last two hours of your shift?" she asked.

Lexi nodded and moved to the next bucket.

"All right, then I'm going to take my break." She shot her another glare. It seemed whatever shaky camaraderie they'd formed was now exploded.

She shook herself. None of it mattered—Matthew was alive. The worst could have happened and didn't.

Ella left on her break, and Lexi sank into the routine of work again. She hadn't been exactly happy at work since the first time Mr. Young had faced her with her mistakes. But she finished her shift and she and Ella set about closing down the shop.

"I'll take care of the register," Ella said.

"Okay." The less Lexi touched it the better. Her self-esteem had hit an all-time low, and she'd messed up plenty in life. She hadn't felt this stupid in a long time, not since that checkbook catastrophe that had sent three of her brothers after her ex-boyfriend, who'd been taking advantage of her.

Ella grabbed her purse from under the counter and looked to Lexi. "I'm ready."

"You go on ahead. I need to use the bathroom before I go. I'll lock up."

"Okay, if you're sure. I'm meeting friends anyway."

"Yes, I've got it. Have a nice time." Thing was that she actually meant it. Ella wasn't an enemy, just a woman trapped in the middle of this mess between Lexi and her boss.

Ella smiled and threw her a wave on her way out the front door. Lexi waited for several minutes before she called Rocko. When she let him in discreetly through the delivery entrance, her eyes slipped closed at the nearness of him.

The bigness of him.

His masculine scent.

She closed the door and turned to face the man.

He searched her eyes. "I guess I have a lot of things to explain."

"It can wait." She stepped up and into his arms. Going on tiptoe, she captured his lips in a searing kiss that melted through her endurance in a blink. She hitched a leg around his hip and rubbed against his thigh, ripping a growl from him.

Cupping his angled jaw, she said, "We'll talk later. Right now, I need you. I've never needed anybody in my life the way I need you."

He slid his hand under her skirt that fell away to expose her leg, nipping at her lower lip. "I can't wait to sink into your tight pussy again, baby."

She reached back for the zipper on her spine and managed to tug it down so her dress hung off her shoulders. A shimmy and she was free of it, standing before him in only her bra, panties and a pair of high heels.

He let out a harsh groan. "Jesus, you're the sexiest woman alive. I'm hard as steel for you."

As he one-handedly fumbled open his fly, she stilled him with a hand. Looking into his eyes, she said, "If you're not up to it... I can do the work."

He shot her a grin, the first one she'd seen since that day he'd taken her before his accident. "Baby, I might have lost an arm, but I can still do pushups with you all night long."

* * * * *

When she reached for the clasp of her bra, Rocko touched the back of her hand.. "Wait—we can't do this here. I wasn't thinking. You'll get in trouble with your boss."

"I'm already about to lose my job. It doesn't matter."

He blinked at her admission. What the hell had gone on here while he was out of the loop? Lexi loved this job. She woke up every morning with a smile on her face because she was coming to work. That was damn rare, and now it was lost?

He'd get to the bottom of it, but first he drew her close again, nuzzling her ear. "There's probably surveillance, and I won't have you naked on tape. Let's go back to my place."

She wiggled against him, curves driving him wild. His cock leaked precum. "There are only cameras on the front door in case someone decides to rob the place. C'mon, Matthew, don't tell me you lost your balls along with your arm."

He went still, and she did too.

She drew back to stare at him with wide eyes. "I-I'm sorry. I should have—"

A laugh bubbled up, unexpected. "Leave it to you to put things in perspective. I'm damn glad I still have my balls. Let me prove it." He lifted her with his good arm, levering her against the wall and pinning her with his hips. Testing his limits and stretching himself into new ones.

He hadn't come here thinking he'd have sex with her, yet here he was, and now he needed to find out just how well he could perform. To say he wanted all those breathy cries of hers was an understatement.

She pulled him down and kissed him, a tender meeting of mouths that soon spiraled into dirty, fuck-me-now territory. She ground into him, and he eased a fingertip inside the leg of her panties to find her slick and ready.

A growl escaped him, and he let her slip down the wall to touch the floor. She went for his shirt, but he stopped her, not quite ready for her to see his arm. She stared at him as if she understood his pause and then moved to his waistband. The moment she reached into his briefs and withdrew his length on her soft palm, he lost all restraint.

"Drop the panties — now," he ordered.

She issued a sound of agreement and rid herself of the silky garment, stepping out of them.

He dipped his stare to her thighs, smooth and sculpted with the running she did. Calves tormenting, ankles turned delicately. And the high heels.

"Grab onto my neck."

She did and he lifted her again. When she wrapped her thighs around his hips, the tip of his erection nudged at her slippery folds. With one shove, he joined them.

Her eyes loomed close, and he saw them glimmering with tears. "I hurt you?" he rasped. It wouldn't be easy to stop but he would, for her.

She shook her head, and her hair drifted around her shoulders and the tops of her breasts. He lowered his mouth to hers again, tasting all the desire on her tongue as she danced it over his. Need tightened his balls, and he drove deep. She cried out and rocked into him.

When he withdrew and fucked her hard again, she bit into his lower lip. The pleasure-pain drove him on. She clung to him, small noises erupting from her as her tight pussy clenched around him over and over. When she dropped her forehead against his on a shuddering release, his need rocketed upward and hot cum shot up from deep in his balls.

Christ, he wasn't wearing a condom.

If he knocked up the Knights' sister, they'd bury him.

She squeezed down on his cock, and he was helpless to do anything but give himself up to sensation, riding the wave of pleasure. After three more spurts, he let out a long groan.

Wrapping her arms tight around him, she brushed kisses over his cheek, jaw and finally his lips.

He gently withdrew from her body. Her eyes widened as she realized he wasn't sheathed.

"Hell. I'm sorry, Lexi. I didn't realize until I was coming that—"

"I trust you. Besides, I'm on the pill."

Relief swept him, followed by a distant thunder of disappointment. He didn't want to contemplate

107

why he might want to put his child in her belly, and he firmly shoved all thoughts of it away.

I can still free her from this… she can walk away and get on with her life.

The very idea gutted him, and he pulled her against his chest once more.

She gave a sniffle, and he used a fingertip beneath the delicate point of her chin to draw her head up to look into her eyes. Sure enough, the depths pooled. "Why the tears?"

"I'm just emotional from… well, the whole day was a roller coaster, wasn't it? You were here, then angry with me, tried to walk away. You did walk away. Then you came back and now…"

He let her go long enough to reach for her dress. He helped her into it the best he could when he was still pretty inept at dressing himself. When he struggled to zip it up the back, she sensed his frustration and turned to look at him.

"It's okay, I can get it. Tyler says I have monkey arms." She reached behind herself and managed to zip her dress alone.

He righted his own clothes and stood staring at her. On the floor between them lay the scrap of her panties. He bent and scooped them up, automatically bringing them to his nose.

She gaped at him, and then a shiver ran through her. "God, that was hot."

A smile tipped up the corner of his lips, feeling as foreign as the other times it had happened since his accident.

"C'mere, baby." He opened his arms and she stepped into them, sliding hers around his waist and pressing her cheek to his chest. "What is going on here at work?"

She sucked in a long, deep breath—and then promptly burst into tears.

He stared at her face for answers, but she didn't respond and he couldn't wipe her tears away fast enough.

"Is there some problem with your boss?" he asked.

She nodded, breath hitching as she tried to control her emotions.

"You said you were about to be fired. What happened?"

When she withdrew from his hold and took several steps away, he noted the slump of her shoulders. The downtrodden set of them hadn't happened overnight—she'd been bearing the weight of something for a while now.

And he hadn't been here for her.

She wrapped her arms around herself and chewed her lower lip for a minute.

"Lexi, let me help you. Please."

It spilled out all at once. "I keep f-fucking up the transactions and giving the wrong change or just doing numbers wrong. You know what a fuck-up I am with math."

"Baby, you're far from a fuck-up."

"Well, I'm on probation and then today there were more problems apparently, and I was hardly even here at work today—I skipped at least three hours of my shift—and I still managed to mess up. Which means as soon as the boss finds it, I'm terminated. And he *has* found it, according to Ella."

"Ella. That girl who was working with you earlier?"

She nodded, and a tear dripped from her chin. "I mean, it's just a job. I can get another."

Except it wasn't, not to Lexi. He stepped up close and pulled her head down on his chest again. The feel of her slightly trembling in his hold ignited the primal urge to protect her, to shelter her.

And to beat the fuck out of anyone who upset her.

"You said there isn't surveillance."

"Right. Mr. Young is kind of old-fashioned, and people don't really come in to steal flowers."

He grunted in acknowledgment but he also believed someone else could be stealing from the till, and it might be missed without surveillance.

"I'll set up some cameras," he said.

She drew back to look up at him. "Why would you do that?"

"Because you said yourself you weren't even here most of your shift yet figures managed to get off somehow. Maybe it isn't you, Lexi."

"I wish that was the case, but no. I've always been terrible with numbers. It's my employee number being entered for the transaction, and there's no way it isn't me."

"Well, I'd still like to help. I can have something set up tonight if you can get me back into the shop."

"I can."

"Good." He cupped her face and kissed her. "You don't have to be alone in this."

She eyed him. "Is that what you told yourself when you were keeping me away from the hospital?"

He deserved that but didn't reply.

* * * * *

The shop was dark and quiet, calming almost. Lexi sat at the desk staring into space, just thinking about everything.

About Matthew coming back to her, not whole, but he would be in time. If the stubborn ass gave her a chance to help him, that was. It was clear his confidence was suffering.

Setting up surveillance in the shop was risky. Her boss would flip when he found out. But Matthew seemed adamant that it could bring some answers, and Lexi would do just about anything to be cleared of accusations.

She thought on her coworker. Ella was far too sweet to be stealing. Besides, it was her uncle she would be stealing from. That didn't set well with most people, let alone someone like Ella.

When the soft knock sounded at the delivery entrance, she stood and went to open it. Matthew came in carrying a bulky box, which he set on the desk.

"Thanks for doing this," she said.

He nodded, not looking at her.

Uh-oh. Was he having second thoughts about her—again?

She moved to stand in front of him. He started pulling gadgets from the box, and she put them back in as fast as he unpacked.

"What are you doing?" he asked.

"What happened since you left me that you can't look me in the eyes now?" She ducked her head to try to catch his gaze, but he evaded her.

He let his arm drop to his side. "We need to talk about what happened."

Her jaw dropped, but she quickly shut it. "Oh no. No you don't. You're not trying to walk on me."

"Lexi, it's for the b—"

"You're not going all man-baby on me. So you lost an arm—boohoo. It's like when guys get a cold and think they need hospitalized or their liver's failing suddenly. You have limbs and a prosthetic that looks like it could launch its own rockets. And your cock works just fine."

It was his turn to gawk. "Just fine?" he echoed.

"Okay, it works great." She grinned and stepped up, rubbing on him like a cat craving affection. In seconds, he was fully hard and kissing her.

They grappled with each other's clothing, and he reached into the box on the desk, pulling out a blanket. She cocked a brow. "You brought a blanket but you were about to talk me out of us again? When are you going to learn that this thing we have is real and I'm not running away?"

Grabbing the blanket, she unfurled it on the floor behind the desk. Then she shimmied out of her panties for a second time and dropped her bra as well.

He stood staring at her in the dim glow of a single light hanging over the door. The way his eyes traveled over her made her feel a rush of exhilaration. It wasn't the ideal location for a romantic interlude, yet the quiet space with the warm yellow glow added a touch of ambience. Add in the lingering fragrance of flowers the shop always smelled of, and Lexi wouldn't complain.

Especially now that he'd added a cozy touch with a blanket.

He reached into the box again and pulled out a second. Then eyes burning, he shucked his clothes and followed her down onto the blanket.

The instant his bare flesh met hers, she forgot the shock of seeing his arm exposed. Passion rose up, along with a huge blast of love for this man.

She put her arms around him, and he stared into her eyes. "I want you in a bed," he ground out.

"At least here we don't have my siblings milling around downstairs."

He huffed out a laugh. "I hardly thought about it after I got you in my arms. Lexi... You're so beautiful. I don't deserve the right to touch you."

"I should smack you for saying that, but I like compliments too much."

He did laugh this time, a deep, rich sound that sprinkled across her skin, leaving goosebumps in its wake. Just having his carved, naked body pressed up against hers had her panting with desire, and she couldn't stop herself from touching him.

When she brushed her lips down his jaw toward his neck, he stiffened. She raised her head. "I'm sorry I wasn't thinking about your injury. Does it still hurt?"

He shook his head. "No, but it's ugly."

Her heart welled with love for him. "Babe, the scars you bear are far from ugly. They're heroic. And I have scars too."

He searched over her.

"They're on the inside," she whispered.

He made a noise in his throat. "Come here." He dragged her atop him, and she parted her thighs to straddled his hips. The hard edge of his cock against her wet folds had them both moaning. Then he yanked her down and kissed her, tongue pushing inside her mouth and claiming her mind, body and soul.

She moved her hand to hold herself up better and bumped his prosthetic arm. It felt odd and foreign, but she moved past the moment without calling attention to it, and soon he relaxed again.

Slowing the kiss, she reached between their bodies and cupped his cock in her hand. The thick length seemed to pulsate, and she traced a ridge of vein running up the side to the mushroomed tip.

"I need you," she said hotly.

His hand met hers and he gripped his cock, angling it toward her center. She sank down, watching his face as he fed his shaft into her pussy. When she was seated fully on him, they stared into each other's eyes.

"Fuck," he ground out.

"Oh, I will." She began to move, using her knees to lever herself up and down over his big body, taking him to the root and then withdrawing almost to the tip before plunging down over him again.

Seeing his face as she drove him higher and higher to the pinnacle of pleasure made her own fires hotter, and she cried out with each thrust.

He planted his hand on her ass and helped her churn her hips faster, taking them both higher. A pinpoint of ecstasy brightened and stretched in her mind's eye, and then she tightened on him and burst on a blinding cry.

Contractions swept over her, and she heard his answering growl as the first splash of his hot cum hit her inner walls.

He flattened her against him and captured her mouth, sinking his tongue in time to his cock, until the final shocks of orgasm faded.

She remained on top of him, breathing slowly as her mind returned and took over once more.

He stroked a path up her spine, leaving small shivers in his wake. Suddenly, she realized she'd never feel both hands on her body... but firmly shoved the thought away. She had Matthew — it didn't matter if he'd lost all his limbs. She loved this man.

He rolled her to the side and drew the blanket over them both. The small circles he caressed on her spine spread warmth through her, and she went boneless in his hold.

Against her hair, he said, "Lexi, what happened to you while I was away?"

She considered his words. Did she tell him how angry she'd been with him for abandoning her? Or was that better left unsaid for the time being? He couldn't totally help it, after all. Though he damn well should have called for her to come immediately.

She moved on to the other worries she'd been carrying the burden of, but she didn't want to tell him that.

"What do you mean?"

"You said your scars are on the inside."

She swallowed hard, feeling the humiliation all over again of hundreds of failed attempts to do things right and frustrations of knowing it would never happen. Because her mind was missing a firing pin or a microchip or something others had.

"It's just work stuff," she said at last.

"Tell me about it. Please." He caught a tendril of her hair between his fingertips and rubbed it.

She looked down into his eyes, wondering how to form the words when they always made her choke up and cry. She hated this part of herself, but how could she expect him to open up to her if she couldn't do the same?

Letting out a breath slowly, she said, "I'm just not cut out for running registers or ringing up customers. I've known that since I was in second grade and Tyler was put into an advanced class to work independently while I sat at a table with the teacher and two other kids. And even then I didn't measure up. It was a fight to get through school, but I came to terms with it."

He nodded for her to go on.

"It's happened throughout my life in different ways, and I just can't stand to see the look of pity on my family's faces when I don't measure up in adult life. Now I'm seeing that same look on my boss's face, and his last straw was pulled and it's time to give me my walking papers."

Her voice wobbled, and she swallowed hard. Then she drew a deep, refreshing breath and stared into Matthew's eyes. "Everyone has to eat a big bag of shit sometime in life. Every single one of us. It's not just me and I don't wallow."

"I know you don't."

Carefully, she reached for his hand. "And you shouldn't either."

He stiffened.

She stroked his knuckles and studied the lines around the corners of his mouth. "The important thing isn't what was taken away from you, Matthew, but what you do with what you now have."

He was still a moment longer and then turned his hand over and grasped her fingers. Clutching them tight and pulling her into his arms again, slamming his mouth over hers.

After dizzying minutes, they surfaced and broke apart. He gazed into her eyes. "I've still got one good hand to finger you with."

"Don't forget a tongue too."

He burst out laughing. "You're the most amazing woman, Lexi."

"And I'm lucky as hell to have you, Matthew." She got to her feet and tossed his shirt at him. "Now, what are we going to do with those cameras you brought?"

* * * * *

As Lexi approached the back entrance of the flower shop, she slowed her pace. And it wasn't only because she was still a little stiff and sore from amazingly hot sex in the back room with Matthew.

She was nervous about Mr. Young or Ella noticing the cameras he'd rigged throughout the front of the store as well as the back room.

The devices were the tiniest things she'd ever seen, yet a business owner would surely notice any little change, right?

Not if it's the size of a bug, Matthew had assured her when she'd asked.

That was in the dark, but in the light of day, what if wires were visible or something stuck out? She'd be in a truckload of trouble if Mr. Young found out she'd taken it upon herself to wire the shop.

She fidgeted with the key and then managed to fit it into the slot. As soon as she opened the door and disarmed the alarm system, she switched on the light and scoped the floor for articles of forgotten clothing. But it seemed Matthew had left with both his shoes last night and for once she had her underwear.

Heaving a sigh of relief, she then started looking for the cameras. She knew one was tucked up under the light and pointed at the desk, but she couldn't

119

make it out even by squinting. Matthew assured her that even if she was fired and never was able to return and remove the cameras, nobody would likely notice them unless the whole place was remodeled. And that probably wouldn't happen in Mr. Young's lifetime.

Smiling to herself, she set down her handbag and turned on the lights to the front shop. The floral coolers hummed away, a sound she'd come to think of as calming.

Out front, everything was in order. Nothing out of place and not a single camera in sight.

He'd done a stellar job. If he decided not to return to Knight Ops — or he couldn't get his skills up to par again, God forbid — he always had a place in security systems.

When she was satisfied all was in order, she went to the front door and unlocked it.

The mornings were always slow, so she expected some time to think on what had happened last night. As she moved through the store, filling water pots and plucking off browning petals, she let her mind wander.

The man still wasn't healed, was far from okay. She had no clue what traumas he might carry, like many vets did. But the bottom line was she was there for him.

When the first customer came in, she greeted her with a smile and then set about helping her choose a perfect premade arrangement for a friend's birthday.

They chatted about the special day as Lexi wrapped the floral in clear wrap and tied it with a huge red bow.

But when she stepped up to the register, she froze. Felt her fingers go numb.

Great — I have my own trauma and it's the silliest of all. I'm hyperventilating over ringing up a customer.

She sucked in a breath and punched in her ID number and then the code for the bouquet size. Then totaled the amount, which automatically added the tax. She couldn't mess this up, right?

It was only in taking the money or giving change where she made errors.

She read off the total, heart pounding in her ears. When she accepted two bills, she carefully did the math in her head and punched in the amount tendered. Her boss at her first job at a fast food restaurant had tried hard to get Lexi to count back change to customers, but she'd never gotten the hang of it and relied on the numbers the computer spit out for her.

She counted the change first — twice. Then went on to the bills. Now her hands were clammy, but what did she even have to lose? She needed to take her own words to Matthew seriously. Life dealt everyone crap, and you had to make the most of it.

Passing over the change, she nodded and smiled at the customer. Then another came in and another. After that, Ella arrived for her shift. Lexi greeted her cheerfully, earning a raised eyebrow from the girl.

But she went on with her day, enjoying working with the flowers and making small talk with customers that she loved.

When she heard the back door open, she knew Mr. Young had come at last. Ella threw her a sympathetic look, which Lexi ignored.

Her boss came out into the front and beckoned her with a hand. "Can I see you a minute?"

Lexi stared at him and nodded.

Her whole life she'd been sheltered by her parents and siblings. Hell, even Rocko had tried to shield her from his injury. Well, it was time to stop saying she could handle her life and actually do it.

She'd hold her head high no matter what happened.

When Mr. Young took her into the back room and had her sit down across from the desk, she wondered how her face looked like on the surveillance. Did it register the pain she was feeling at being let go?

Mr. Young compressed his lips. "I'm sorry I have to do it, Lexi. I've enjoyed having you on staff."

She gave a slight smile, determined to hide her tears until she was alone. "Thank you, Mr. Young. I've enjoyed it too. Now what do you need from me? My keys, I'm sure." Her voice was a touch too cheerful, and he looked at her closely.

She ignored him and dug around in her handbag for her work keys. Those she passed across the desk with another smile. She stood and faced her boss. "I'll stop by for my paycheck next week."

"All right," was all he said.

She extended her hand. He shook it. "Best to you," she said, feeling her world crumbling at the same time she battled for some sort of upper hand, even if it was only to keep from breaking down.

"To you as well, Lexi."

As she passed the camera, she put on a mask to cover her pain. It was bad enough she'd shared her problem with Matthew, but the last thing she wanted him to see was how crushed she really was in spirit.

Chapter Seven

Rocko pulled into the base parking lot and put his SUV in park. The last time he'd been here, he'd discovered Lexi's panties on his passenger's seat, and that had set off a chain of events leading up to now.

Lexi... Somehow he had to find a way to be the best man for the job.

Since parting from each other last night, he'd thought of her nonstop. This morning she'd already be at work, and he couldn't wait to check the app on his cell to look at the surveillance. Whatever was happening at the shop, he didn't believe she was suddenly making mistakes. But her self-confidence was at a low, and hopefully installing the cameras would give her peace of mind.

He got out of the vehicle and looked toward the building. The Gulf breeze washed over him. He breathed deep.

Same wind, different man.

He faced the building. Something told him he was about to meet his biggest fear—Jackson hadn't called him in to talk about his golf handicap.

As he approached the door, the guard gave him a nod and smile. "Good to see you, Rocko."

"You too, Manning."

"Back in the swing of things, I see. Most respect for you."

"Thank you." He'd gotten that a lot lately, and it made him think twice about words he'd said to other men like him, men who'd been shot down, put out of commission. *Respect for you, brother.* He meant those words and these guys did too. Yet somehow he didn't totally feel the pride he should and wondered if the other vets didn't either.

There was always that question dangling in the back of his mind—could I have avoided making this error that cost me my arm? How could I have done things differently?

He entered the building and started down the long corridor leading to Jackson's office. The long walk wasn't one he'd ever enjoyed. It either meant he was getting his ass chewed or was being sent someplace he didn't want to go, but he would because it was his duty.

Fuckin' Mississippi. He might have chuckled if he didn't miss his team so badly. What he wouldn't give right now to be with them, holed up in some godforsaken place trying to put a stop to some threat.

His chest burned as he entered the colonel's office. Snapping to a salute, he was thankful once more that he hadn't lost his dominant hand.

Jackson stood and saluted back. "At ease, Rocko. Sit down."

He took the seat, bracing himself for the words he never wanted to hear—honorable discharge.

For a moment, the colonel just looked at him, gaze traveling over his arm, shoulder, up to his face. "You've regained your health, I see. Good."

"I've worked hard, sir."

"Not without its challenges, I'm sure. But you're not a hundred percent."

Rocko looked down at his prosthetic, still feeling the ache of his lost hand and those severed nerves that may or may not ever stop hurting. "No, sir."

"You might have been told there's a training program. In San Francisco."

"Sir?"

"A return to basic training, if you will, but for men like you."

He imagined a whole regiment of men with fake limbs fighting to get back on top of their game. He winced at the thought but quickly masked it from Jackson.

"I'm sending you, Rocko. We need you—Knight Ops needs you. And we think with a little honing, you'll be back full force or even better than ever. Are you up to the challenge?" the colonel asked.

Rocko sat for a long moment, processing the question. Mostly because he wasn't sure he *was* up to it.

Then he thought of Lexi telling him that we all have to eat shit sometimes. Leave it to her to open his eyes with language more blunt than any Marine's.

Well, he was finished having a taste of that shit.

"I'm ready, sir. And grateful for the opportunity." He was suddenly choked up. This was a new chapter of his life. He'd flipped a page and found himself staring at a new road that would lead him back to the old team that was his family.

And Lexi would be so proud of him again.

"When do I go?" he asked the colonel.

"There's a flight leaving at 0900."

He let out a breath. That soon. OFFSUS constantly operated on a timeline that was cutting it so close they barely had time to throw clothes into a duffel bag before they were shipping out.

No time to talk to her, to tell her he loved her. Maybe that was for the best—a long goodbye would only hurt her further, and after what he'd done... Well, he'd fucked things up enough for a lifetime.

Giving a nod, he said, "I can be ready in half an hour."

"Good news, Rocko. And good luck." That was as good as a dismissal from this man.

Rocko stood and gave a salute. His insides shook with excitement and apprehension. He was new to this life with a prosthetic arm, and he didn't know if he could keep up with the others in the program, who might have more time to get accustomed to the change in their bodies.

And he was damn nervous about leaving Lexi.

When he got into his SUV, he glanced at the seat but no red slinky panties lay there waiting for him.

He took out his cell and debated for a long minute about calling her. But that would mean tears and a lot of leave-taking, and he'd told Jackson a half hour. He had time to gather his belongings and make his flight.

As he backed out of the spot, he realized something had to be said to someone. He dialed Ben.

"What's up, Rocko?" he asked immediately.

"I think you know."

A beat of silence and, "You're going then?"

"Yes. I don't have much time."

"Shit. You don't have time to talk to Lexi, do you?"

"No." Ben also didn't know—unless Lexi had told him this morning—that he'd returned to her and stirred things up in a big way. "Look, I saw her last night. Things are fucked up at the flower shop."

"Wait—Lexi's shop?"

"Yes. She doesn't want anyone to know what's going on."

"Dammit, is she being targeted again? Who is the bastard?"

"It's not a man." He almost laughed, because he was the guy the Knight brothers would fuck up if he broke Lexi's heart again. "There are some mistakes being made and she was put on probation. She thinks she's going to be fired soon for making errors."

"Goddammit."

"She's a wreck but she's proud and she won't admit to needing help. I took matters into my own hands."

"What do you mean?" Ben's voice rang with suspicion.

"She let me into the shop last night after hours and I set up surveillance. I don't have time to monitor it now, though. I'll give you the code to access it."

"I'm waiting."

He knew his captain would be standing there without pen or paper, prepared to lock the numbers and letters into his mind like a steel vault to pull out at the exact moment he needed them. They'd all been trained this way, had to be prepared for anything at any moment.

He recited the code, and Ben grunted. "Got it."

"Thanks."

"I'll take care of her."

"I know you will, but..."

"But what?"

"I'm damn sorry for the way I'm leaving things. I don't have time to say goodbye."

"I'll make sure she knows."

He battled with emotion, for the woman he loved, for her brother who was like his own family, always there for him. "Tell my sister Chloe too. You have her number." They'd never discussed the fact that he'd gotten hold of his sister without Rocko's permission. Now he was glad he'd pulled Chloe into his life when he needed her.

"You're welcome for that too. Now focus yourself on the task at hand so you can come back. We're getting sick of your replacement. He farts up a storm and the Knight Ops-Mobile stinks."

He laughed at the problem as well as the reference to the SUV they traveled in like a pack, squabbling over who got to pick the music or whose turn it was to empty the trash from the back seat.

He made a fist with this prosthetic hand and brought it to his heart. "Guts and glory, man."

"All the way. See you when I see you, asshole."

* * * * *

Lexi sat on the back porch, staring into space. Not seeing the pretty gardens she and her mother liked to tend or the yard her father griped about cutting so often.

She was heartsick.

And now heartbroken.

Matthew Rock, it seemed, had skipped out on her again.

She'd called him. Gone by his place, and finally called the rehab center asking if he'd been checked back in.

The man was nowhere to be found, and where did that leave her?

Snatching up her phone, she stabbed a button that would reach Ben. He answered first ring, and all the bottled emotion shot out like a cork. "Rocko's gone again. The jerk came to find me and then tried to walk away. Can you believe that shit? He went months without telling me where he was and what had happened—made you guys keep it from me! Then he fucking comes back and tries to say that what we have is over and didn't mean anything."

"Lexi, calm down."

"No, I won't calm down. Because I convinced him—or thought I had—that I don't care if he has a fake arm or scars because I love him anyway. You have a problem with that, take it up with me, Ben Knight." Her voice sounded with warning.

Was he chuckling? She pressed the phone tighter to her ear.

"Calm down, sis. It's going to be all right."

"Easy for you to fucking say. Your wife's safe at home and God fucking knows where my fucking man went. Oh wait, he's not my fucking man!"

"Okay, only I'm allowed to drop the F bomb that many times. Lexi, I'm coming over to talk to you right now."

She opened her mouth to let loose another explosion and then realized what he'd said. In a quiet voice, she said, "You're coming over?"

"Yes. Sit tight and wait for me. Don't say fuck in front of *Maman* either. She'll lose her fucking mind."

That brought a small laugh from her, though she didn't feel a bit better. She hung up and waited, drawing her knees up as she sat on the lounge chair, watching clouds drift by and replaying everything Matthew had said to her in parting that might have given some indication he was separating himself from her for good.

A few minutes later she heard the crunch of tires on gravel and knew Ben had arrived. Her brother came around the side of the house and stepped onto the patio.

She glared up at him. "What is it you know?"

He shook his head. "You're the biggest hard-ass of us all, Lex. If you weren't such a sweetheart, I totally believe you'd have me at knifepoint trying to get the information from me."

She eyed him. "I can still go find a knife. *Maman's* got a good sharp carver."

He laughed and sank to the lounge. She wondered if the legs would support both of them—her brother was huge. But it didn't so much as creak.

Ben looked into her eyes. "Lexi, I know what happened with the flower shop."

132

She expected to learn Matthew had left Louisiana for good and had given up on Knight Ops. That he'd confided to Ben that he'd made a mistake and couldn't face her.

But she hadn't been expecting that.

She got off the chair and walked several paces away. He watched her, concern slashing his brows.

She wrapped her arms around her middle. "He told you?"

After she'd confided, he'd turned around and told her brother?

"Lexi, he had to." He stood and came to face her, putting his hands on her shoulders. "He's worried about you but he had to leave quickly and asked me to—"

She sucked in a sharp breath. "He's gone?"

"To San Francisco. A short program to refresh himself so he can rejoin the team."

"Oh God." She dropped her face into her hands. "I'm such a selfish fucking idiot."

Ben made a noise that sounded like part amusement at her language and part sympathy. He pulled her close and held her. "You're not an idiot, and you have a right to feel things haven't been perfect with whatever relationship you're trying to have with Rocko."

She dropped her hands and gazed up at him. "Perfect? I'm just asking for him to stick around and stop leaving me out of the loop. But this... He needs it."

"You know, when Rocko took that hit..."

She looked up at Ben's face, holding her breath. She knew almost nothing about what had really happened that day, but felt she needed to in order to support her man fully.

Ben went on, "He kept trying to get up. Trying to... reach for his weapon with an arm that wasn't there anymore. We had to pin him down to keep him from battle. He needs this, Lexi. He loves what he does."

She nodded. It was best for him to go and train to be what he was before. He was going to return to the work he loved.

She couldn't say the same for herself. She'd been looking at job ads in the newspaper half the afternoon and realized all she was qualified to do was wait tables. Which she had to if she wanted to retain her sanity. If she sat at home all day, she'd only end up arguing with her mother about who was fixing meals or cleaning up.

She pushed out a sigh through her nostrils. "I'm a selfish person."

"You aren't. And Rocko would understand. He was really upset knowing he couldn't speak to you before leaving."

"Will he be able to call eventually?"

"I don't know. It's treated like a stricter basic training."

Her hopes fell. "So six more weeks without him?"

Ben nodded. "Unfortunately, yes. But I'm here for you. We all are. We'll distract you, get you to babysit for me and Dahlia."

She stuck out her tongue, and he laughed. "I love my niece and no offense, but that isn't the distraction I was hoping for."

"I know, *cher*." He hugged her. Then quietly, he said, "I can help you with your problem too. I have access to the surveillance Rocko set up."

She gulped. "You do?"

He nodded.

Pulling away, she plopped back onto the lounger. "Fat lot of good it does me. I was fired this morning, Ben. It doesn't matter if I messed up or something else was going wrong. I'm out of a job."

* * * * *

Smoke rolled off the grill as the cook pressed a thick Cajun-spiced burger down on the hot metal. Lexi stuck the order slip up on the carousel and called out for her next order.

"Comin' as fast I can, Lexi," the cook replied.

"They've been waiting for twenty minutes."

"Well, it's lunch hour. Tell them to hold onto their asses or go get a fast food burger."

She pressed her lips into a firm line and turned away from the window, looking out at the jam-packed restaurant. Why she'd chosen this one to work at, she had no idea. After a week, she'd realized she was in over her head.

Not because she couldn't juggle tables or get orders straight. But because the place was old-fashioned, having their waitresses write up all the receipts manually, which meant Lexi was not only faced with too many tables but too many numbers on the bills.

So far, she'd managed to throw out as many, "Write that up for me, would you, doll? I'll refill all your coffees if you do," as she could. But times like these, the waitresses were just as slammed as she was, and she had to write up her own damn slips.

She also had to deal with assholes like the ones waiting on their burgers.

The four guys came in daily, even on weekends, and she swore it was just to harass the girls who worked at Cajun Dan's. When her fellow waitresses saw them walk through the door, they gave each other pleading eyes until one would give in and take them to her section of the restaurant.

Today happened to be Lexi's day. She'd taken them in exchange for Dawn writing up three of her slips. But now she was wondering if it was worth it.

Arming herself with more coffee, she sidled up to their table. The guys gave her looks like they wanted to eat her up. Every time she waited on them, at least one would ask her to go into the bathroom with him.

Not one for putting up with men's shit—she had five brothers, after all—she always shot them down with her sharp tongue, which had earned her respect from the other waitresses.

Still, she didn't want to deal with them anymore.

"Order's just about ready. Sorry for the wait."

"How 'bout you entertain me, sweetheart?" One reached out as if to grab the curve of her ass. She danced aside.

"How 'bout you go down to Bourbon Street and find a hooker?" she shot back.

The other three guys laughed, but the one offending her wasn't put out. He grinned. "Someday I'll get you, sweetheart."

She topped off one coffee. "Only thing you'll get from me is my foot up your ass." Then smiling sweetly, she walked away.

Steaming inside.

Dawn shot her a grin.

"Six up," the cook called out.

Damn. She had to walk back over there with their order so soon? She circled the room again, refilling coffees before making her way to the window. As she gathered the plates into her arms, balancing them expertly, she fortified herself for round two.

"I never got this sort of disrespect in the flower shop," she muttered.

When she approached their table again, the most belligerent asshole of the group started harassing her right away about the quality of the food. "Probably cold. Looks cold. Doesn't that sandwich look cold?" he asked his buddy.

"She looks hot to me. Oh, you mean the food."

She set the plate before the man. "The plate's steaming hot. I'm pretty sure the food is too," she said.

The guy nearest her tipped his head, examining her legs in her shorter skirt she was required to wear as uniform. Freakin' Cajun Dan realized the lure of sex appeal in his workers. It was half of what kept the place packed. That and the burgers piled with all the fixin's, including seasoned shrimp.

"You're a runner, aren't you, Lexi?"

She ignored him and plopped a plate on the table in front of him, then moved to the next. She'd learned early on not to lean over to serve—they enjoyed looking down her cleavage.

"Those look like runner's legs to me. Mmm-hmm." He didn't remove his stare from her thighs.

"That's right. I'm a great runner. I know how to run far away from chauvinist pigs like you." Smiling sweetly again, she walked away to hoots of laughter.

God, how degrading. She took their slip and went to the register. There, the menu with prices was spread out for the waitresses to use in writing up their bills and the calculator was taped down to the counter.

She set about recording the prices. Then looked it over, checking each and every number, which sometimes turned backward for her. When she discovered a nine and a four reversed, she scribbled it out in blue ink and switched them.

"Lexi, you're up!" came from the kitchen.

She felt that old familiar pressure of the clock ticking down the seconds to the end of a test, and she still had several more problems to do.

She began punching the figures into the calculator. The number she got looked okay. Not too much. But was it correct?

"Lexi, table thirteen!"

"Dammit, I hear you." She hated this job. Tucking the slip into her pocket, she bustled back across the restaurant to the window, dropping the bill off at the asshole table of four on the way.

After checking that their meals were fine, she went about ignoring them and actually had a pleasant conversation with an older lady who came in often for gumbo.

"Hey, this check's incorrect," one of the assholes said to her on the way by.

She stopped, feeling heat climb her cheeks. "I used the calculator."

"Well, you didn't use it right, sweetheart. It should be thirty-nine, not forty-two. You trying to overcharge us so you can get a bigger tip?"

Her face scorched. Her throat clogged off with rage and angry tears.

Dawn reached past her and plucked the slip from his hand. "I'll double-check it and take off the drinks to make up for it."

Lexi's heart pounded. Great. It was happening all over again, and now the other girls were going to try to cover for her.

As far as she knew, Ben hadn't seen anything weird from the footage in the flower shop, and she assumed everything really had been her fault, after all.

But how had she managed not to screw up for years? Or had she been making errors all along and it just took that long for Mr. Young to find them?

"Took care of it. Don't worry about a thing, Lexi." Dawn stood at her elbow.

She turned to offer a forced smile. "Thanks," she said brightly.

When was she going to be able to stop faking everything in her life? Faking that she liked her job, was doing fine here. Faking that she didn't ache for Matthew.

And wasn't worried as hell that when he returned, he'd forget all that had happened between them and ditch her for good.

Chapter Eight

Water lapped at the deck supports, and Lexi closed her eyes, letting the calm of the bayou sweep her away. Each time she came to the family cabin in the Boondocks, she thanked God that her parents had built it for all of them to enjoy.

Over the years, it had served as party house and retreat, family fun center and personal place of solitude. Right now, she was happy to have two days off in a row from waiting tables to pull herself together.

The peace and quiet the first few hours always seemed strange to her, but she cradled her glass of wine and looked out across the trees dripping with Spanish moss and the occasional gator eyes popping up in the swamp.

Two blissful days alone. No rat-race of pouring coffee and dishing up pie. No cook calling out orders.

No asshole table.

It also meant no thinking about the flower shop and what her regular customers were saying about her absence.

Okay, here she was thinking about all those things instead of unwinding.

She dragged in a deep breath of the tangy air and imagined she smelled smoke from her father's grill as he dropped a slab of steak onto the seasoned metal. Too many memories here to count, each different and just as special as the last. Add in the times Rocko joined them and there was no way Lexi could ever dream of not coming to this place.

She brought her wine glass to her lips and sipped the light rosé. Her mother kept the bottle here in her personal stash, but *Maman* wouldn't mind her sneaking a bottle.

She stretched her legs out, feeling the sun kissing along her shins. She couldn't stay out for long without burning and—

Tipping her head, she listened. Was that the wind playing tricks on her as it bristled through the Spanish moss or did she detect the splash of an oar?

Automatically, she looked toward the head of the bend, and sure enough, one of the family canoes came into sight. She leaped to her feet, nearly spilling her wine, and braced a hand over her eyes to dim the blaring sun.

Just making out the outline of a man that could be any one of her brothers. Broad-shouldered and sitting up far too high in the vessel to be anybody but a Knight boy.

"Dammit." There went her solitude. So much for peace and quiet. She knew her brothers extremely well, and none of them ever shut up, especially now that they were married. They took every chance possible to boast about their married lives. And Tyler was equally as bad, relaying stories of all the fun she and Hawk had.

A groan slipped past Lexi's lips as she made out exactly which brother it was. Ben was the worst of the lot—he'd be needling her for information about her feelings and talking out what had taken place at the flower shop.

She sucked in a breath. The shop. He had the code for the surveillance. What if he was here to bring her news?

Setting aside her wine, she moved to the end of the deck that surrounded the cabin on all four sides and watched as her brother's strong arms propelled him quickly through the water.

As soon as he could see the whites of her eyes, a grin plastered over his face. He lifted a hand in greeting.

She waved back and after he drifted the last few feet to the dock, she bent to grab the canoe while he tied it off.

"What are you doing here?"

"I see you aren't wasting time getting to the point." He tossed his duffel onto the dock and stepped out after it. Before he said another word, he drew her into his arms. The big, comforting embrace made her annoyed and misty-eyed at the same time. Damn him for coming, yet she couldn't think of anyone else she'd rather see besides Rocko.

"I thought you might bring news of the surveillance."

He pressed his lips into a firm line. "No, I'm sorry, Lexi. I've gone over that footage a coupla times and I'm not seeing anything odd taking place."

Her shoulders slumped. She'd known it, of course. It just sucked to hear.

"Thanks for looking out for me. Any news from Rocko?" she asked.

"Nope. He'll be tied up a while longer." He nodded toward her glass of wine. "You got anything heavier around the place?"

"You know *Papa* has his stash of gin."

He made a face. "Hate gin. Let's go see what else we can rustle up."

In the end, they found a half a case of beer hidden in the back of the fridge, which Ben announced served him just fine. Lexi watched him make a thick sandwich using the ingredients she'd brought with her. If he kept eating this way, they'd be out of food in hours, but she didn't remark on it.

When he sat with a plate and a beer to eat, she stood back sipping her wine and contemplating him.

Finally, he looked up. "What?"

"I'm just wondering something."

"You might as well ask."

"Did you tell any of our other siblings about my problem with work?"

He looked up, gave her a deadpan stare and said, "No."

"Oh good." She circled him, and he put down his sandwich to keep an eye on her. "You didn't let it slip to anyone else?"

He hesitated. "I might have told Chaz."

Chaz. That was better than she could hope for. She and Chaz and Tyler were close, being so near in age. Growing up, she and Tyler would play princesses and Chaz would be the horse pulling their wagon carriage. At least until their *maman* demanded to know how he'd so thoroughly ruined the knees of his jeans.

She circled to his side and leaned down to look him in the eye. "Only Chaz."

"Might have been Dylan too. I think he was there, yeah."

"Uh-huh. Of course he was. And at that moment Sean and Roades came by."

"Nope." He picked up his sandwich and bit off a big bite.

Relief swept her.

"They came later."

She straightened and threw her hands in the air, spilling her wine. "So you told all of our brothers when I specifically told you I wanted to deal with the problem myself."

"You have to understand, they're our brothers but they're also my team. It's difficult to keep anything from each other."

"Dammit," she muttered then pierced him with a glare. "Brothers. That means you didn't let it slip to Tyler."

She looked at his face.

"You did."

"Yes, but I didn't tell Hawk."

"Jesus, Ben, you don't have to! Tyler will do that for you. So the entire family knows I was fired and why. Thanks a lot. It was already humiliated enough."

"Oh Lexi." He set aside his sandwich and stood to grasp her shoulders. "You never have to be anything but yourself with us. We love you, you know that. We only want the best for you, and we want to help in all ways."

"Nobody can help me get that job back, and now I'm stuck at this horrible restaurant serving obnoxious guests on a daily. Forget it. I need more wine." She strode to the fridge where she had the rosé chilling. She poured a full glass and drifted back to the table, taking the seat adjacent to Ben. But just then the sound of laughter carried through the open windows, seeming to sail across the kitchen.

The familiar voices of her brothers and... yes, Tyler too. When she ran outside, she saw the boats and old pirogue paddling up to the dock. Sean was already climbing out, a smile on his face for her.

"Hey, sis. Sorry to hear about your troubles." He planted a kiss on her forehead.

She grunted in irritation. Not only was her secret not a secret anymore but her solitude was wrecked.

By the time they all hit the deck with bags and a big cooler full of food between them, it was a full-blown Knights party.

"I'll fire up the grill," Chaz said, striding for the old junker their *papa* preferred.

"I'll season the steaks," Roades added, tossing a smile Lexi's way. "Hey, kid. Doin' all right?"

"Uh..." She had no idea how to respond to such a question.

Dylan punched her lightly on the arm as he passed hauling the cooler with a grin for her.

Then Tyler stood in front of Lexi, and the sympathy in her eyes was too much for Lexi to bear.

She raised her glass to ward off any sisterly hugs, though it was the exact opposite of her usual desires and somehow she and her twin had managed to switch roles.

Tyler came in for the hug anyway. She smelled of fresh shampoo and sunblock. Lexi couldn't help herself from bringing her arms around her sissy.

"Aww, see? It's all going to be fine. We're here now." Tyler wore this glow from within, as she had since the moment she'd hooked up with Hawk.

"If you say so."

"I do."

"Then you know I say it's time Hawk puts a ring on that." She waved at her sister's bare finger.

She waved back. "Neither of us can wear rings anyway with what we do. We're thinking more along the lines of matching tattoos."

Lexi gasped. "A hipster wedding!"

"Oh God."

"It's perfect! You're both unconventional and Hawk is so stylish, I bet he'll love the idea."

"Glad to put a smile on your face, Lexi."

She brought her fingers to her lips and stifled a giggle. "I came here to be alone and think, and now I'm thinking this is exactly what I needed."

"Family?" Tyler hedged.

She gave an enthusiastic nod and grabbed her sister's hand. "Let's get you some wine."

"Who wants wine when you can have margaritas? I brought mix."

She looked at the deck where Chaz had gotten the charcoal lit in the grill and the other guys were drifting out onto the dock with beers while Ben complained from inside that they were drinking it all.

Tyler grabbed her hand. "We're not letting you do this alone, sis."

They'd brought more than food, drink and entertainment. They'd brought Lexi comfort she hadn't even known she needed.

* * * * *

One trans-humeral amputee, two bilaterals, a below-elbow limb loss, one leg at the knee and Rocko. He ticked down through their ranks. The amputees in the training were the hardest workers he'd ever had the honor of working with.

It also made him feel like a weakling when he was exhausted by the physical effort it took to match his old moves. But he kept his mouth shut on any complaints like the rest of them.

The shooting course was spread out before them, and the guy with the leg prosthetic tapped his new limb sporting the laser-printed American flag and grinned at the group. "I'd say I've got the advantage at this sport." Then he wiggled all ten of his fingers.

"Shut up, Newhart. Wait till you need to crawl through pig shit," the only woman among them retorted. Her face was good-natured, but it was a deception. She was a hardcore robot of a soldier, and so far she'd whipped each of their asses at one thing or other.

Their captain approached the group. "Stop whining, you babies, and grab your ammo."

Rocko was most nervous about the target test. He'd fucked up plenty, even sent off a wild shot or two, which had earned him dozens of pushups and a hell of a lot of ribbing from the others. But it was all helping to push him to a better skill set. If he wanted back on Knight Ops, he had to be able to perform.

No way was he setting foot on that team unless he could defend them all a thousand percent.

The guy with two partial arms reached for his weapon and ammo with a precision that had Rocko worried. He wanted this win above any other. He could do plenty of pullups and didn't need more skill climbing ropes — he had all he needed. But this was his game.

"Line up," the captain ordered. "You're taking turns, one at a time running the course. When you've reached the end, your time will be given to you, and I will walk through myself to record your scores."

"Loser buys us all a steak dinner," Newhart said, obviously feeling cocky.

The petite but badass Lieutenant Cara Volks eyed him up and down. "Get ready to pull out your credit card, because I'll be ordering the sixteen-ounce ribeye."

Ignoring the banter, the captain lifted his chin toward Rocko. "You're up, beautiful."

Rocko looked at the others and whispered, "Should I tell him I have a girlfriend?"

Laughter followed him as he headed to the start of the course. Twenty targets. Some popping up out of nowhere, relying on speed and reaction time. Many distance shots that would require most of his attention as he attempted to balance and stabilize his weapon using his new limb.

And he was beginning to think of it as an extension of himself. Not quite there yet, but he could see how in the years to come he would begin to feel it was almost normal.

He loaded his weapon and lifted it to his shoulder, staring down the scope.

The captain held a stopwatch in his own prosthetic hand. "Go!"

He took the shot. Hitting dead center. Crouching as he turned the corner to the next, which was a man target bursting up in front of his face. At point-blank range, he shot it between the eyes and then dodged something flying his way. He dropped and rolled, coming up onto one knee and firing again.

Maybe Newhart would struggle with that one, but the man was solid. And Rocko was glad to call them all friends.

Again and again he moved through the course as fast as possible. He felt he was flying through it and maybe should slow down, but he was aiming true and hardly thinking about the weapon being steady. Maybe all those hours at the range had given him the boost he needed.

The final target loomed before him, and damn if it wasn't putting him in an awkward position for his new body.

He rested his shoulder against a wooden beam and calmed his breathing. But the beam pressed against the joint between what remained of his shoulder and the titanium arm. It slipped.

The gun rolled in his grip and a roar rose up. No—this was not taking him down.

He slammed his shoulder hard against the beam and took the shot.

It hit exactly where he was aiming.

After they'd all finished the course, they stood around waiting on their scores, which didn't seem to be forthcoming. A new commander stood in front of them, eyeing them up in total silence.

Rocko was reminded of his first day of basic and how he'd believed himself to be tough. That day he'd discovered he wasn't—not yet.

"Hope you got your stamina up, crew, because you're running."

Newhart bounced on his foot and prosthetic. He'd been training for this. And Rocko had too. He'd never found running to be such an outlet. It gave him time to think and put things in perspective.

Like his relationship with Lexi.

He'd been a dumb ass, trying to hide from her and then push her away. She deserved so much more, but he was damn well going to live up to his end of the bargain and be everything she needed.

"Ten miles, commander?" one of the guys asked, making a face.

"Yeah. Quit your bitchin'." He lifted both pantlegs to show two prosthetics. Rocko's throat closed with utter respect and admiration. An arm was bad enough but both legs? He wasn't sure if he would be here right now, trying again.

As they were given the flag to begin the run, his mind eased into thoughts of Lexi. The beauty owned his damn heart, and as soon as he got back to Louisiana, he was grabbing her up and telling her.

After he kissed her breathless, that was. The mere thought of her lips under his had a burn forming low in his groin, and he couldn't run with a hard-on. He pushed the image of his lover away, but she came back full force.

Had Ben learned anything from the surveillance? Best scenario, she wasn't making the errors she hated to admit to. It had damn near killed her to tell him about it, and the tears standing in her eyes as she did so still speared him in the heart.

But he was here for her, would help her stand up to any challenge. She didn't want to come up short in any way, and if anyone understood that, it was him.

As he stretched his legs into the second mile and then the third, he hit his rhythm and got up to speed. Didn't that little peckerhead Newhart pass him, though. As he went by, Rocko gave him the finger and Newhart's laughter trailed back to him.

His muscles burned. His body hummed with the pleasure of exertion. He was going home soon to rejoin his team.

To be with the woman he loved.

He was happier than he'd been in a long time.

Chapter Nine

"Earth to Lexi." Dawn snapped her fingers in front of her face, snapping her out of a daydream.

She looked up at her friend.

"Your order's been up for a while. Didn't you hear the cook calling your name?"

She shook her head and moved automatically to the window. As soon as the cook saw her, he rolled his eyes. "Better get on the ball, girlie. Boss won't keep you around if you start delivering cold food to customers."

She stiffened. She'd had enough of reprimands for a lifetime. Somehow, she'd managed to keep from making money errors when she wrote up the slips or else the other girls were kind enough to do them for her. So far, she'd kept her problem with numbers off the radar, and she wanted to keep it that way.

Loading her arms with plates, she carried them to the table and smiled and chatted with the customers about their meals as she set them before them. From the corner of her eye, she noted the assholes slipping in the door and being led to one of their usual tables in the back.

Today the other waitress on shift with her and Dawn would get them—good, because she'd had a stomach-full of their crap over the past week.

As she turned away, one guy called out to her. She pretended not to hear him and rotated between tables, checking her customers. She picked up a stack of bills left as a tip and pocketed it in her apron. The cash was almost better than the flower shop, though that didn't make her enjoy it any more.

She missed the artistic part of the job as well. Since being fired, she hadn't even touched a flower, which was sad when it was such a big part of her life before.

Even her mother had commented that they had plenty of flowers in the gardens if she felt like cutting some for arrangements for the house. Lexi didn't know if she missed seeing the beautiful bouquets that had dotted the rooms before or if she recognized the melancholy in Lexi.

"Ugh, they're in rare form today," Dawn whispered as she passed her.

Lexi paused and threw a look at the back of the restaurant where Kyla, the other waitress, was trying her best to handle the crap the guys dealt her.

"Couldn't they find any puppies to kick today?" she asked Dawn.

She groaned. "Guess not. Little old ladies either."

"I'm getting sick of their crap."

"Aren't we all?"

They looked to Kyla, who was dancing quickly away from hands that would grab.

"Why doesn't the boss ever kick them out?"

Dawn raised a brow. "I dunno. Maybe because he's a male too and doesn't see it as any big deal? Either way, we're stuck with them."

"Unless I could dump hot coffee in their laps and burn off any reason to come back." Lexi's blunt statement had them both giggling.

Then they both had orders up and broke apart to do their jobs.

Kyla passed by Lexi, face burning red. Lexi put out a hand. "You okay?"

She groaned. "You wouldn't believe what those assholes said to me."

"I can guess. Want me to take over? I'll still give you the tip."

"Nah, I can't run from jerks like that. It's like putting up with a catcall on the street—you have to be ready with a good comeback that shoots them down."

Lexi nodded. As women, none of them should have to deal with that behavior.

She watched Kyla closely. Anger was building inside Lexi for the young girl—for all of them.

When she saw Kyla jump away from the table as one obviously grabbed her thigh, Lexi slammed down the coffee carafe she was holding.

"What are you doing?" Dawn asked nervously.

"If the boss won't kick them out, I will." She stormed up to the table. Again, Kyla's face was scorching red, and Lexi didn't have to look closely to see tears in her eyes.

"Oh, it's Miss Sexy Short Skirt, guys. Come to give us some of that paint thinner you call coffee? Why don't you go make a fresh pot for us, sweetheart?"

"Why don't you shove your dick up your own ass and fuck yourself?"

Kyla's jaw dropped, and heads whipped at her words.

"Excuse me? You're treating a good paying customer this way?"

Lexi planted a hand on her hip. "I'd say you guys are neither good customers or paying. Half the time you're complaining so much that you get most of your meals free. Why don't you go down the block and find another restaurant from now on?"

One guy with a shaved head raised his eyebrows, which caused his entire scalp to move. Tyler would have found that hilarious and she and Lexi would have had a good giggle over it. But right now, Lexi didn't think anything about these guys was remotely funny.

"I'm serious—settle up your bill and leave. Don't come back."

"You're kicking us out?" The guy raised his voice and stood at the same time. "Everyone, this waitress is throwing us out of here. We come here daily—"

"And grab our asses," she interrupted.

He threw her a dark look. "And spend our hard-earned bucks here."

"Or not because you say the buns are stale or the burgers overcooked. The shrimp's not fresh. The coffee's not hot. Oh, and it tastes like paint thinner." She ticked things off on her fingers.

From the kitchen, she saw the cook come out. "What's going on here, Lexi?"

"These guys are making Kyla uncomfortable. One of them grabbed her."

The cook's brows lowered. "You harassing my girls?"

"Every day," Lexi said.

The cook waved a hand at the door. "Get out, like she says. We don't need your breed here."

All four guys were on their feet, glaring and tossing down napkins. They didn't bother to pick up the bill and headed to the door.

"You forgot to pay for the food you ordered," the cook called out.

One guy whirled, face screwed up and fist balled. He took a swing for the cook that never reached him, because Lexi shot up a hand and compressed the nerve in his neck. His knees buckled as he lost consciousness, and he tipped forward onto the floor.

Someone screamed, maybe Dawn. Lexi glared at the other three guys. "Carry his sorry ass out of here. And don't come back. You can leave the money on the counter on your way."

They hesitated.

Lexi sighed. "Look, I've got five siblings in the Marines and special forces. I know a lot more moves if you'd like to stick around and try me."

Two guys gave her wary looks as she gathered up their buddy and carried him out, one bearing the weight of his chest and one with his feet. The fourth straggled after them, tossing down bills on the counter before they walked out the door.

Total silence followed. Then suddenly a cheer went up.

"Holy crap, Lexi, did you kill him?" Dawn asked, rushing up.

She didn't know whether to laugh or cry. She'd never used force against anyone in her life, but she was glad her brothers had taught her those tactics to use if her life was ever in danger.

She never dealt with this sort of crap working at the flower shop.

"Good job, little lady," a guy at a nearby booth said. "I listen to them several times and week and the place will be much better without them."

Kyla came up and hugged Lexi. She squeezed the girl back. When she released her, the cook was waiting with his palm up for a high-five. But the minute she slapped his palm, he grabbed her for a hug too.

Several people clapped for her, and she dipped her head, feeling more embarrassed than she ever had as she picked up her coffeepot again and continued serving tables as if nothing at all had happened.

Maybe she'd done some good here today — preserved a waitress's self-esteem or kept the cook from getting a black eye. But it didn't make her feel any better. She wished she had the calm of the flower shop, her nose filled with beautiful scents rather than Cajun spices.

And if she was honest, she wished she had Matthew here to fold her into his arms and tell her she'd done well, that it was normal that she was still shaking even half an hour later.

Maybe her family pampering her for all those years had made her a wimp. Because right now, all she wanted was for someone else to step in and tell her how to get out of this mess that had become her life.

There was no water left in her emotional flowerpot.

* * * * *

Rocko stepped up to baggage claim and grabbed his duffel, shouldering it in the same move. Next to him, a gentleman looked over his camo, his army green bag and his wounded warriors ballcap and gave him a nod.

"Thank you for your service."

Rocko'd heard it before, but this time his throat closed off. He nodded back in thanks and headed out of the airport. Only one thing had been on his mind for weeks — getting home to his girl.

He'd left her at the worst possible time, and he felt like a huge ass because of it. He also wasn't sure what to expect from her. Either she'd be his sweet angel, supportive and happy just to see him again, even if he had gone without notice. Or she'd be the tough gal who would plant a hand on her hip and give him a telling off that would shrivel his balls.

The corner of his lips tipped up. He hoped it was both — they were equally adorable. If she was feeling nice, he could persuade her to come to bed easier. If she wasn't, well… he was up for the challenge.

Transport was waiting for him, and he slid into the passenger's seat. The private drove away from the curb and was filling him in on the latest mood of Jackson's. It seemed he'd asked his girlfriend to marry him and he'd gone soft on everyone around him.

Rocko laughed at that. "I doubt he's gone soft. Give him a week to recover. He'll be back to his hard old self."

When they arrived on base, Rocko climbed out and threw the private a wave on the way to his vehicle.

"Can't get you to join us for drinks?" he called.

Rocko shook his head. "Another time. Gotta go see my girl."

What had she been doing with herself while he was away? Mardi Gras had come and gone, and now the heat of the city was in full force. As he drove down the streets, he saw girls in shorts and sundresses. Which brought to mind a certain sundress that had finally made him lose all control.

As he drove, his mind wandered to happier times to come. He was fully trained and ready to lock and load. Knight Ops would have him on the road again before he even knew it.

He just hoped to hell he got some time alone with Lexi before he was called out.

Lexi... Seeing her again, staring into her eyes and seeing the love reflected there...

He let out a sigh and drove straight to her house. It was early enough that he'd catch her before her shift at the flower shop — if she still worked there. Again, it bothered him more than anything that he hadn't been here for her.

Her words had echoed in his head over and over during the course of his training. *My scars are inside.*

Knowing her, she'd spent a lifetime slapping a smile on it, giving a positive twist to her frustrations. While at his lowest point, when he struggled to do all the physical things he once had, he'd thought of Lexi. Her limitations were inside and out of her control, and he couldn't imagine the fight she'd had to put up her entire life.

He also knew how much she hated being watched over or babied by her family in any way, so the fact that she'd confided in him, let him in for a brief second, made his love for her well up even more.

When he got her in his arms again, he was going to spill out everything in his heart for her. It was past due.

* * * * *

Lexi lay in bed, staring at the cell phone in her hands and in a bad mood. Dawn was sick and asking her to take her shift. Of course she would—she helped everyone—but she wasn't eager to put on her public smile today.

She replied to Dawn that she'd take her shift and then shut off her phone and rolled onto her side. Staring at the window framed by thin draperies with small pale blush-colored roses on them, she thought, This is my life. It's all I have.

A tear rolled down her cheek to wet her pillowcase, and she wasn't proud of it, but she couldn't stop it from falling either. Times like these, she tried to be thankful for everything she had—health, a roof over her head and a great family.

It seemed losing the things that kept her going in life had let the air out of a balloon, though, and she couldn't stop feeling sorry for herself.

Others would tell her to get up and fight for what she loved. To find another flower shop to work in. Dawn had even suggested she go on a dating app after hearing about Rocko.

But she wouldn't do either. Matthew would be back, and she could only hope that when he did, he'd be able to go on and wanted her at his side.

Another tear escaped from the corner of her eye. She let it go and the one after it too.

The crunch of tires on gravel had her wondering who was coming by the house this early. Usually deliverymen didn't come until afternoon.

She levered herself up to peer out the window.

Her stomach gave a wild lurch, and then she was off the bed and running for the bathroom. Dragging her fingers through her hair, she simultaneously scrubbed her teeth and then rinsed with mouthwash.

By the time her feet hit the stairs, she heard Matthew's voice. She careened to a stop at the foot of the steps, and her father gave her an amused glance.

But she only had eyes for the beautiful man in front of her.

"Matthew," she breathed.

"God, you're a beautiful mess." He stomped across the room and she hurled herself into his arms, tears flowing as she clung to the man she loved and had missed more than even she'd allowed herself to admit.

She heard her father quietly leave the room.

He caught her chin and lifted her face to meet her gaze. "Happy tears I hope?"

"What do you mean by mess?"

He laughed. Locking his fist in her hair, he tipped her head all the way back. Then dipping his lips to her throat, he murmured against her skin. "You've got just-fucked-me hair."

Liquid heat soaked her panties, and she quivered in his hold as he slowly moved his lips up and down her throat. When he paused over her tripping pulse, she gasped out.

"You're home now? For good?" she managed to get out as he worked his way over the point of her chin to hover with his lips over hers.

So close and yet so far away.

How was it he was bigger, harder, more muscled? Whatever they'd done to him in training, it had made him into a beast.

Her sexy beast. And she couldn't wait to straddle him and slide down over that thick length of his cock again.

"Till Knight Ops needs me, I'm here."

She met his stare. "Good, because I need you."

He claimed her lips. Delving his tongue deep, stealing all the noises she couldn't help but make as he molded her body to his. When he wedged his thigh between hers, she rubbed wantonly against it.

"Jesus, I'm going to lose it with you in this itty bitty nightgown. Your parents are home."

"*Papa's* on his way to work and *Maman* will be over at Dahlia's helping with the grandbaby. Take me to bed, Matthew." Her soft words came out as a plea, and she couldn't deny the desperation she felt to feel his mouth on her, his tongue, hands… cock inside her.

Before she got a thought out, he swept her into his arms, legs dangling over his prosthetic arm. Worry hit that he wasn't able to support her weight all the way up the stairs but she quickly forgot about that when he lay her on her rumpled bed.

He groaned as he lay her down. "Your sheets are still warm from you. God, Lexi, I've missed you." He buried his face against her neck.

She wrapped her arms around his broad shoulders and savored the feel of him at last. "I've hardly thought of anything but you. Matthew, does this mean… you being here… Are you finally admitting we're in a relationship?"

"Baby doll, I'm marrying you. Don't even think about fighting me on that."

A whoop left her, and she threw her arms around him tighter. Kissing with all the passion and joy filling her.

Quickly, their kisses spiraled out of control and she was shocked to find herself naked and sprawled on the bed beneath him. In his glory—ripped muscles, battle scars and all the help OFFSUS had provided to make him whole again—she stared at him and tears came to her eyes.

"I love you so much, Matthew."

He sobered as he stared down at her. "You'll forgive me for the way I acted? Trying to blow you off, avoiding you? Then leaving for the last training when you needed me most?"

She swallowed hard against the knot in her throat and nodded.

"And your job at the flower shop?"

"It's gone. But it doesn't matter because I've got you." She pushed upward, urging him inside her.

It didn't take much coaxing—she was wet, he was steely hard.

When he sank to the hilt in one long stroke, they both cried out. Need blasted through her, heightened by all the love she felt, and in three jerks of his hips, she felt her insides clamping down on him.

The inner tremors began, and he swallowed each noise she made until his groaning joined the sound. Together they came to a rapid release and kept moving, kissing, rolling, groping.

He pressed down on her clit with the big pad of his thumb and caressed her into another hasty orgasm that sucked the breath from her.

Panting, she stared down into his eyes and began to ride his still hard cock for another round. "Let's hope the world doesn't fall apart just yet, because I need you more than Knight Ops right now."

Latching onto her hips, he guided her up and down in a slow roll that sent lust pounding through her veins. His eyes burned with love and desire. "Even when I'm away, I'm all yours, baby doll. And I'm going to make you come for me again."

He threw all he had into reaching that perfect spot and in minutes, she was tossing her head back on another cry. Humming with pleasure, happier than she'd ever been.

She was about to start a new chapter in her life.

Chapter Ten

"Lexi." Rocko stared down at her lovely face, flushed pink from the countless orgasms he'd just given her. She bore red marks on her throat from his stubble and quite a few on her inner thighs too, which she hadn't yet noticed.

She opened her eyes and looked at him, her full lips tilted into a smile.

She was so stunning and peaceful, he hated to bring up bad thoughts, but he had to know.

"What happened with your job?"

Her expression fell. He clasped her fingers and stroked her knuckles with his thumb.

"Exactly what we thought would happen. I was at fault."

"Ben didn't find anything on the footage?"

She shook her head. "I take it you haven't seen my brother."

"I came straight here."

That made her smile, and he returned it, heart full. But he was still aching over her obvious unhappiness concerning her job.

"Have you been working?" he asked.

She stared at a spot on his chest. "At a restaurant."

"And you're not happy."

"It's all right. The girls are nice."

He heard the hesitation in her voice and didn't know if he should ask about her making errors on other money transactions as she'd been accused of at the shop.

"What's happened?"

"Well." She giggled. "There were these guys I threw out. And I might have assaulted one."

His jaw dropped and he jerked back to stare down into her eyes. "What?"

She filled him in and pretty soon he was laughing.

"They haven't been back since?"

"No." She giggled again, the sweetest sound in the universe and one he longed to hear from her lips as often as possible.

"As much as I don't like the thought of anybody fucking with my woman, I'm glad you grew up with five tough brothers."

"Don't forget the sister."

"That too." He rolled to the mattress and cuddled her close. The rise and fall of her chest grew more even and he realized with a touch of ego that he'd worn her out.

However, he was wide awake, and his brain was racing over the things she'd told him. Could he do anything to help her get a job she loved again?

Even if her name was cleared, working for the old boss didn't seem like a good option. The minute the register was a penny off, she'd be scrutinized, and that wouldn't do, not for his Lexi. He could easily support her, if she'd let him. Thing was, she'd never be satisfied staying home.

He did want to clear her name, though. Something just felt off about the entire flower shop deal.

He had to see that footage for himself. Right after he held his lover while she slept. He needed her to regain her strength so he could make love to her again.

* * * * *

There was a definite bounce in Lexi's step, despite the fact she was going to take a shift at the restaurant even on her precious day off. The cat nap she'd taken after Matthew's intense lovemaking had restored her.

It also set the wheels of her mind turning.

She passed by a homeless man and gave him some of the dollar bills she kept in her pocket for this walk to work. Then she slowed her steps, considering Matthew's questions about the flower shop.

She never had gotten all the information from her accountant friend. It was time she called him again and see how he'd made out with the computer printout. More than likely, he would have contacted her if something had been amiss, but still, she had to know.

As she walked the last block to Cajun Dan's she gave him a call, and he agreed to meet her at the restaurant before her shift ended. Then she tried to call Matthew — her fiancé, how crazy was that? — and only got his voicemail.

A worry that he'd been called away on a mission had her phoning Ben. When she couldn't reach him, she went down the list of brothers and finally pocketed her phone, cussing.

They were called away, that was obvious. Worry weighted her final steps to the door of the restaurant. This would be Matthew's first mission after his injury. What if he couldn't handle it?

No, he was in great shape — better than before. He could make good use of that arm too — he'd picked her up and carried her to bed like it was nothing.

When she walked in, Kyla gave her a double glance.

"You're blushing. What happened?"

Oh Lord, was she? She patted her cheeks. "It's getting hot out," she said, but Kyla didn't look like she bought it.

The work kept her busy and her mind off the worst of her worries about Matthew. But in the down times, she had a lot of concerns about his mental health, his ability to battle through.

If she lost him…

She'd come close, and she was so lucky that she hadn't. Still, how did her sisters-in-law or even her own twin who was married to a special ops man deal with this crap? She'd be asking them as soon as she saw them. Now that she knew how Matthew felt about her, she couldn't lose him. They had their lives to build together.

Thing was, she had no clue what to expect there. From living arrangements to how to split up responsibilities when her spouse would be away from home so much, she had no ideas. Then there was the strangely blank mind she had when it came to thoughts of her own wedding.

For a person who loved helping with her sisters-in-law's events and even her own sister's, this detail surprised her. But she couldn't envision the dress, rings, venue, flowers… nothing.

Not a big deal by any stretch, but still confusing.

By the time she was wrapping up her shift and refilling salt and pepper shakers, she glanced up to see her friend Brett making his way to her. She set down the shakers she was holding and turned to him with a big smile and open arms. They embraced.

She waved toward a booth. "Take a seat. I'll get us some coffee."

"Sure."

When she returned, she noted that he looked less strained than last time she'd seen him. Either he was getting over his failed marriage or something had changed on that front. She wasn't going to ask, but was happier for him.

After she slid into the booth as well and poured their coffee, they faced each with another smile.

"You look well."

"You look better," he said at the same time.

"Oh," she said. "Last time we met was quite a roller coaster. I'm sorry for that."

"You got things straightened out?"

She beamed. "I'm getting married."

He stared down at her hands on the table.

"I don't have a ring yet. He just returned from a military training and hasn't had time to get me one yet."

"He must be really special if he's put that smile on your face. I hope I get an invitation?" Brett arched a brow.

She laughed. "Of course. And you? You look happier too."

He lifted his coffee and took a sip. Then he leaned in and whispered, "Not as good as the coffeeshop's coffee."

She nodded. "I know."

"Anyway, I'm making some big changes in my life. I quit working for the firm I was with. I realized my stress there probably contributed to me losing my wife. But that has only forced me to move forward and take a risk I never would if I had her to think of."

"What's the risk?" she asked, sipping her own coffee, which though fresh and hot, wasn't the quality of the coffeeshop where they'd met before.

"I'm moving to Miami and opening my own accounting firm."

Her mouth opened in an O of surprise. "Brett, I'm so happy for you. That's great!"

He nodded. "I love New Orleans, but I'm ready for a change of scenery and the challenge of my own business. Now." He set his hand on a folder he'd brought with him. "I bet you want to know if I found anything."

She nodded.

He chewed his lip. "I haven't. I'm sorry, Lexi. It seems all the affairs are in order."

The letdown wasn't as painful as she expected it to be. Though she slumped a bit in the seat, she'd known it was coming. "I figured as much. I appreciate you taking a deeper look for me."

"I wish I had better news."

"You know, I wouldn't work for Mr. Young again anyway. I just hoped for my own closure."

Brett nodded, contemplating her. "Have you considered branching out on your own like I have? Closed doors mean new ones open, after all."

She blinked at him. "I... No." Her mind whirled. "I've never thought about having my own business, because, well... We both know how I am with numbers. I can't run a business without great bookkeeping."

"You can hire people for that."

"Where would I even get the funds to start?"

"Well, I know personally that you're amazing at what you do, and maybe you could just hire yourself out as a wedding flower designer. That only involves using someone else's funds for the upfront costs. You could put the arrangements together in your garage to begin and later if you enjoy it, expand."

She simply stared at him. "Brett, I can't believe you're saying this to me."

He sobered. "I'm sorry if you think it's a bad idea. You don't have to take my advice."

"No, I mean, that you think someone like me could own and operate my own business."

It was his turn to look surprised. "Lexi, you can do whatever you want, be whatever you want. There are millionaires who never completed high school, you know that. I've told you before. And many creative people have someone with business sense standing at their backs to help them."

Suddenly, she thought of Dawn. Of how the woman was quite clever with running things in the restaurant that many waitresses didn't. She handled the food deliveries and the ordering. She also did payroll at the end of each week. Cajun Dan relied on her, and that was exactly what Brett was talking about.

It seemed too easy.

A dream, far off, seen through the clouds. But still out there, a possibility and a hope.

Plus, she had Matthew to think about now. Anything she did would affect him as well.

When she considered talking to him about this new venture, she could only see how animated he'd become, knowing she would be happy.

By the time she and Brett took leave of each other, she had an even brighter outlook on the world. Nothing could bring her down now.

* * * * *

Last time Rocko was cut off from his team, he'd gotten himself blown the fuck up.

Well, that's not going to happen a second time.

"Two on my six and nine. Fuckers have me hemmed in," he whispered into his comms unit.

"Fuck," came Ben's characteristic foul-mouthed response. "We're moving in now. Sit tight and don't do anything dumb, man."

"I never do anything dumb." Especially now that he had something so much bigger to live for. Before, he had his buddies, work he loved and even his sister, who had come when he needed her most even without his consent.

And now Lexi. He had to get out of here in one piece in order to take her ring shopping. Something told him she wouldn't want something new and they'd spend a week haunting antique shops for the perfect fit. Something vintage yet flashy, that was his girl.

Straining his ears, he listened to the men breathing not far off. He could take down one easily, but that would mean the second would shoot him before he could think twice. He needed that backup and fast.

A scuff sounded, but it was enough.

He whipped toward the noise. Identified his target and took the shot.

Goddammit, I missed.

How, after all the target practice he'd been through over the course of weeks, had he forgotten to shift his supporting arm a bit farther to the right?

"Fucking hell!"

"Rocko, you good, man?"

Inner fury boiled up and over. His first mission back and he'd not only gotten himself cornered but then screwed the only shot he had.

"I'm fine," he grated out. It was a waiting game — to see who would take another shot.

He wanted to jump up and unleash on the guys pinning him down, but...

Lexi. He couldn't take the chance with his own life. It wasn't only him he had to think about anymore. Did the other guys all feel this way too? They had to.

He couldn't even fathom how he'd feel when he had kids to go home to.

Thinking fast and furious, he shot to his feet, swinging around and firing again.

Again, his bullet missed its mark.

"What the fucking hell's happening over there, Rocko? Get the hell out," Ben yelled into his ear.

But he wasn't listening, stunned and irate that he'd somehow fucked up again.

Then a complete and utter calm washed through him.

He could do this. Because his beautiful little woman got up every day of her life and tried again too.

Focusing on his training, he pulled up and took a third shot at the man running.

The man hit the ground, sliding.

A bullet whizzed by Rocko's head.

Rocko laughed and simply took aim at the second threat. After he pulled the trigger, he drawled, "Area secured. No one's taking me down again."

A cheer went up, but it was short-lived, because it was game on and everyone was engaged. Guts and glory.

* * * * *

Rocko cracked open an energy drink and chugged it. Then he crushed the can in his fist and let it drop to the floor of the SUV as he looked out the window at the scenery passing by.

Next to him, Chaz eyed him.

"Don't say a damn word," he said. "I fucked up and I know it. But y'all aren't firing me from this team. It won't happen again."

Silence reigned in the vehicle. Then Ben cleared his throat. "Dude, if you think you're the only guy who misses a shot on occasion, you're crazy. You were shootin' blind, for one. We know damn well you didn't have a clear view let alone a good rest. It could have happened to any one of us."

"It shouldn't happen to me. It won't again."

"Shiiiiit," Chaz drawled. "Maybe they gave him a bionic brain too. The man doesn't think he's even human now. I suppose they put a computer chip in your brain along with giving you that arm." Chaz nudged him.

"Dickhead." But he almost smiled.

"Even snipers fuck up, with or without all their real limbs. Now quit being a whiny baby and let's celebrate." Ben whipped it off the road into the parking lot of a steakhouse. "It's on me."

"It better be because I'm on a budget," Rocko said. "Got a weddin' to pay for."

You could have heard a mouse turd drop.

181

"You proposed to our sister?" Sean asked, twisting in the passenger seat to look at him.

He gave a single nod. "I love her. And I'll fight any of you who objects."

Another beat of silence and then they all burst out laughing. Chaz's booming laugh had Rocko staring at the man, who had tears of amusement leaking from the corners of his eyes.

"Rocko, I take that back about the computer chip in your brain. You're not smarter at all. If you think any of us ever gave a damn if you married Lexi, you're dumber than we thought. We know you've been head over heels for her for years. And she hasn't made it a secret she feels the same."

When Ben drew the vehicle to a stop, they all piled out. As soon as Rocko's boots hit the ground, the guys were on him, delivering light punches and hooking their arms around his neck to draw him in for bro-hugs.

Then Roades planted a kiss on his cheek and welcomed him to the family. Grossed out, Rocko took a swing at him, and some pushing ensued.

Ben opened the restaurant door and waved them inside. "Six for a celebration," he told the hostess, whose jaw dropped at the sight of six huge Marines walking in together. Ben looked to Rocko. "My buddy here's marrying our sister."

Heart full with affection, Rocko clapped Ben on the back. "I'll do right by her."

"'Course you will. Because we'll beat the shit out of you if you don't."

Chapter Eleven

Lexi sat in her car observing the neighborhood where Rocko lived. Between his career and spending time with the Knights, the man wasn't here that often. But she had to admit the up-and-coming area had potential as a place to live.

The houses were older with an occasional new construction where a gap had been missing on the street. With flags flying and inviting porch stoops to sit on and have a neighborly chat, the area had an old-town charm you just didn't see in all parts of New Orleans.

She watched two women pushing baby buggies as they jogged behind. People came out to fetch mail or let their dogs run around the small patches of yard to do their business.

Normal, everyday people. The very citizens that Matthew and her family members were sworn to protect at all costs.

With the car window down, the light breeze washed across her face, bringing a few notes of music from down the block where a couple kids sat on a porch, heads together looking at a tablet screen.

If Lexi married Matthew, she'd be doing her part too, sacrificing time with the man she loved so he could go off and save the world. But she was ready for that, more than willing.

The sky was changing colors, and the clouds lowering. A rain tonight. Wouldn't it be nice to lie in bed naked with Matthew and listen to the whisper of the rain on the windows and roof?

When the SUV turned onto the street, her heart leaped. She hurriedly rolled up the window and got out of the car just as Knight Ops drew up in front of Matthew's house to drop him off.

Ben cut the engine and they piled out. Lexi's heart flooded with love for her brothers, and she reached for her oldest. Ben put his arms around her and squeezed.

"Thank you for texting me to come," she said softly into his shoulder.

He nodded. "He might need you."

She pulled back and smiled at him. "He does."

Ben grinned. Just then the rest of her brothers crowded onto the sidewalk in front of Matthew's place. She looked from face to face, loving each so much that she'd never be able to express it in words. She'd just have to find a way with deeds.

But her gaze lit on the one man who spread a glow over her.

Matthew stepped up onto the curb, and she threw herself into his arms. He pulled her off her feet and found her mouth, kissing her boldly in front of her five brothers. A show for all that he was claiming her.

She squealed when he pinched her bottom.

"That's enough of that," Ben said in his best commanding tone.

They pulled apart and Matthew set her on her feet. Lexi felt flushed all over—embarrassed to be kissed in front of her family, excited for the future... and totally aroused.

She couldn't wait for her brothers to go home to their families and Matthew to take her inside.

"You called her," he said to Ben.

"Figured we'd end your first day back on a high note." He clapped Matthew on the back. "Glad to have you back on the team."

Matthew didn't look away from Lexi as the other guys called out farewells. They piled back into the SUV and drove off.

He chuckled and then ran his fingers through his hair. "Glad to be out of that vehicle. Stinks worse than it did months ago."

"I can imagine. I've been on road trips with my brothers. Still, nothing beat Tyler's feet when she took off her shoes."

He laughed and then sobered. Linking their hands, he said, "Come inside."

She nodded.

He led her up the sidewalk, giving her such a feeling of homecoming that her chest burned. The house was large enough that it was split into two apartments, and his porch was identical to the one next door, except he didn't have any pots of flowers.

Something she could remedy.

He punched in a key code and opened the door, throwing a glance back at her over his shoulder. "I left it kinda messy."

She moved into the entry and he closed the door and locked it behind them. Standing back, he watched her take in her surroundings.

Old wood floors, worn in places but nothing a coat of varnish wouldn't fix. Pairs of boots were kicked off haphazardly on a mat against the wall and the small entry opened into the living space. She could totally envision him lounging on that tan sofa watching the game.

"I can almost read your mind."

She looked up at him with a smile. "What am I thinking?"

"You're already putting your feminine touches on the place."

She smiled wider. "Will we live here then?"

"Maybe till we can find a place farther out in the country. Maybe close to your parents or brothers?"

"None of us are that far away, and I'd like to keep it that way." She turned to him and took his hands.

Gazing into his eyes, she said, "I only care about being with you, Matthew."

His throat worked. "I'm okay, you know. They didn't need to call you to come."

"I would have rendered them all unconscious if they hadn't. And I know you're okay. You're the strongest man I've ever met."

He made a noise in his throat.

"Don't believe me?"

"Plenty are stronger than me."

"Oh, I don't know. Takes a strong man to resist my charms for more than two years."

His face split into a grin, and her heart exploded with love for him. They reached for each other at the same time. Chest to chest and hip to hip. He lowered his mouth to hers slowly and with a gentleness that brought a quiver to her insides.

Their lips melded with a kiss as deliberate as one they'd share on their future wedding day. Then all at once, he yanked her in. As she gasped, he plunged his tongue into her mouth and she climbed him, hitching her thighs around his waist as he began walking toward the bedroom.

In small mutters between thrusts of his tongue, he gave her the tour as they went. "Kitchen. I'll make you eggs in the morning. Office. Don't look — it's a mess."

She giggled and slashed her tongue across his, raising a rumble of need in his chest as he paused at an open door.

Holding her suspended in his arms, he drew back to look into her eyes. "The place I'll make love to you right now."

"And a lot more times to come," she added.

He let her slide down his body. Her feet touched the floor and she kicked off her shoes. Then taking two steps back, she reached for the buttons of her blouse.

"I always loved you in red."

She smiled and drew apart the blouse to reveal her bra.

"And blue," he added, eyes darkening.

She tossed aside her top and dragged up her skirt to show off the matching panties.

"Oh yeah, really love the blue."

She turned, giving him a nice view of her ass as she dropped the skirt over her hips and stepped out of it. She made a show of bending over to collect the garment and drape it over the side of the bed, where she knew it would get crumpled as soon as they hit the mattress.

"Damn, woman. That ass of yours. I plan to worship it all night long."

"I hope so."

She caught the widening of his eyes as she wiggled her backside. Pivoting again, she gave him a come-hither stare. "Your turn."

* * * * *

It was a sort of test, and he knew it. She wasn't trying to see if he'd gotten better at using his prosthetic to remove his clothing—she wanted him to show her all of himself. Every inch in broad daylight and withholding nothing.

He might still have some things to work on, like not fucking up several shots the way he had today, but he was more adept at managing daily tasks. He pulled off his shirt first, casting it aside. Reaching for the waist of his cargo pants, he worked the belt and fly using his prosthetic hand.

Watching her face closely, he recognized a joy in her followed by pride... and ending with her eyes lidding with pleasure as he drew his thick cock from his briefs.

He gave it a deliberate stroke, precum beading at the tip. What he didn't expect was for her to drop to her knees before him, latch onto his hips and wrap that beautiful mouth of hers around his cock.

He shuddered with pleasure and sank his fingers into her soft hair. With light pulls of her mouth, she dragged moans up from the depths of his soul and blew his mind at the same time.

"Lexi. Baby doll, stop or I'm going to blow."

"Mmm-hmm." She flashed her eyes up at him.

He wrapped her hair around his fist and drew her head back. She released him but flicked out her tongue over the slit in his swollen tip.

"Who said good girls can't give head?" he rumbled.

She rose to her feet and removed both bra and panties with a slow deliberation that had him edgy as hell. "I don't know. Never heard such a thing."

He laughed at the expression of false innocence on her lovely face and made quick work of removing the rest of his clothes.

He grabbed for her. Tumbling her onto the bed, hauling her up to place a pillow beneath her head while he kissed her until she was writhing.

She took his hand and placed it on her breast. They shared a noise of need, and he began to caress the firm globe, running his fingertip up and over the crest. Her nipple beaded harder at his touch.

He raised his head. "Time for what you deserve."

"Hmmm. What is that?" Her last syllable cut off on her cry of delight as he sucked on her nipple. Laving the bud until it was straining and small squeaks erupted from her lips.

He slipped his hand down the flat of her stomach, through the small tuft of curls covering her mound. Then he buried two fingers in her soaking wet pussy.

Liquid heat engulfed his hand and ran upward. He pressed his fingers higher, feeling her inner walls clench and quiver.

Releasing her nipple, he sucked at the other while fucking her in long, slow strokes of his hand. She gasped with each plunge and sighed on each withdrawal. Her thighs fell apart, giving him total access. Which was good for what he had planned next.

He kissed a trail down between her breasts, over her ribs and across her navel that had tormented him on countless occasions when she paraded around him in a bikini.

When he stuck out his tongue and traced a path over her mound to the small nub that was just begging for his attention, he looked up into her eyes.

"Taste me," she whispered hoarsely.

God, this woman was such a mix of everything he never believed he was worthy of.

He hovered with his lips over her pussy for a long second, inhaling her scent and stretching out the moment.

When he snaked his tongue over her wet seam, she threw her head back and cried out his name.

* * * * *

Lexi was melting into the bed. Her thighs wrapped around her lover's ears as he sucked and licked every inch of her pussy while thrusting two fingers in and out of her.

She rose and fell on the mattress, aching to get closer to the heat of his mouth and to drive his long fingers deeper. Needing his cock, but not yet.

"So… close," she panted.

"Mmm," he hummed against her sensitive flesh.

He opened his mouth wide and tongued her fast, taking her upward so fast that all she could do was curl her fingers into his hair and hold on for the ride. When the pleasure ripped through her, she bucked up and shook apart.

Juices coated his fingers and lips and jaw. She floated on a haze of extreme ecstasy as he slowed his movements. Licking her softly in short nudges of his tongue and pulling his fingers partway out of her. Which only made her throb more.

She opened her eyes to find him staring at her with such an expression of love that tears salted her tongue.

"Come here," she whispered raggedly, still trembling from her astonishingly strong orgasm.

He moved up her body, dropping kisses on her skin as he did, and when he claimed her mouth, she tasted her release on him.

"Come into me. Come in me," she begged, dragging him close. The tip of his shaft brushed her folds and then he was buried deep.

She flexed around his invasion and gripped his shoulders as their kiss spiraled out of control. "You're not perfect. I'm not either. All that matters is we do this together."

He lost the rhythm and stared down at her. "God, you're my everything." He bucked hard, moving her up the bed with each thrust. Harder and harder, his grunts of need combining with her whimpers of pleasure.

When he moved disjointedly and stiffened, she threw herself into kissing him with abandon. His mouth opened over hers and he poured his hot cum into her. Hips jerking faster as her second release ripped through her.

After what felt like minutes of floating on a fevered haze, she realized that his gaze had never left hers this entire time.

"I love you," he said as he collapsed to the bed.

She rolled into his arms. "I love you too."

Seconds ticked by as they regained their senses. He recovered first, stroking her breasts again and immediately making her nipples hard and aching for more.

"I have a feeling we're going to make the most of that honeymoon."

She giggled at his words. "Where should we go?"

He looked at her. "I thought you'd have all the details planned out already."

She glanced at him a little shyly. "Is it weird that I can see how to plan other people's special days but not my own? I think I need more input from you, Matthew. Are you willing to help?"

"I'll do anything you ask. I'm at your total and complete mercy, my love." He kissed her knuckles and then sucked her fingertip between his lips.

She moaned. Before he swept her away on another tide of pleasure, she wanted to make sure he understood something. "You know I'm here for you, right? That you can't push me away no matter what happens to you."

He studied her. "It can be hard sometimes. But I swear I'll try to open up when I need to and let things go."

"I'll always be here to listen."

"And you have to agree to share your worries with me too."

She sobered.

"You try to act like you're invincible, that nothing bothers you. But I know better. You beat yourself up over your shortcomings, and I won't allow that anymore. It's part of who you are, and I aim to help you work over those hard times. But you have to let me, Lexi."

"I don't suppose saying stubbornness runs in the Knight family is a good reason to not share with you?"

He chuckled and kissed her soundly. "Nope. I know how to deal with you Knights."

She snuggled closer, and he counted her even breaths, more at ease than he'd been in longer than he could remember. Finally, he had all he needed.

* * * * *

When Lexi entered the bedroom fresh from the shower and wrapped in a towel, she saw Matthew sitting on the side of the bed, hunched over.

Her stomach dropped as she slowly approached. "Everything okay, babe?"

He looked back at her and lifted his cell phone in his hand. She glanced at the screen only to see some odd movements of video footage.

"What is that?" she asked.

"The video from the flower shop. I know Ben watched it, but I just wanted to..." He trailed off and drew the phone closer to his face. "Wait. I need to look at this in HD."

He got up and walked into the living room. She trailed after him in only her towel, amused that this would be life with a man like Matthew. Always something urgent or exciting.

As he rigged the video to project on the flat-screen, she watched. Even missing his arm and bearing more scars, he was still beautiful.

He tossed her a look and found her staring. "You admiring me, baby doll?"

"There's a lot to admire." In only his briefs, his tanned muscles made her want to start at the top and lick her way downward.

"Damn, you're turning me on in that towel. But I have to look closer at something." He focused on the TV, and she followed his stare.

Seeing the shop she loved made a hollow widen in her heart, but she forced herself to think of the good times spent there and how it gave her hopes for a future in the same industry. Something she still needed to discuss with her fiancé.

The camera showed the front counter. She came into view, bustling back and forth as she obviously helped a customer. Then Ella was in sight. She leaned against the counter for a while filing her nails as was her usual habit. Then he switched cameras and the register came into plain sight.

Fingers tapped the numbers.

He stopped the footage. Rewound it.

Fingers tapped the numbers.

"Goddamn," he drawled.

She stared at him. "What?"

"See that?"

"Yeah, Ella's fingers. So?"

"So watch the numbers she hits." He rewound it again and slowed the video.

As the numbers registered in Lexi's brain, her blood ran cold. Then hot with fury.

She whipped around to face Matthew. "That's my user number!"

"Yep. I knew hers from watching her enter it a few times. 0-0-3-9."

"And mine's 1-9-2-2. Completely different."

"Uh-huh." He looked into her eyes. "This can be tracked on the printouts. The time here." He tapped the bottom of the screen. "Will be in the system and you'll know if she rang that up wrong."

"To get me fired," she whispered.

"Or to create an overage so she could take the excess cash."

Lexi's jaw dropped. "You think Ella was stealing? From her own uncle?"

"Seen stranger things in my time."

"I know you have." She plunked down on the couch, in shock and disbelief. She shook her head. "I can't believe she'd be taking money, but..." She gasped.

"What is it?" He stared at her.

"She always kept her purse under the counter but we were supposed to keep them in the back room."

"And yours always was in the back room?"

She nodded. "Do you think if she was taking money, she still is? Mr. Young would surely find that easily, especially since he didn't hire a second person to replace me."

"My guess is she was lifting the cash on and off whenever she worked there during her school breaks. Then took on more hours and figured more cash could be slipped out. Except it backfired on her and she got you fired. You were her cover, so she can't embezzle anymore."

Lexi sank against the sofa back, mind awhirl. "So I didn't make all those errors. I mean, I probably made some. I'm not perfect."

"Nobody is," he added.

She met his gaze. "No." A second passed, and then she said, "Now what?"

"Well," he sat beside her, "what do you want to do about it? Confront Ella or take this to Mr. Young?"

Clearing her name would feel damn good. But since she was distanced from the whole drama, she just wanted to keep on trucking. Move on.

Biting her lip, she shook her head. "I think I'll just let it go."

He arched a brow. "You're certain? This could get your job back."

"I..." This was the perfect time to bring up her discussion with Brett and get Matthew's feedback on starting her own business. As she filled him in about her last talk with Brett, he listened intently. When she got to the part about starting her own business, he finished her sentence for her.

"—and you'd be great at it. I already know that, baby doll."

Tears sprang to her eyes. "How could you love me so much and be so supportive of me?"

He made a noise deep in his throat. "You're my world, Lexi."

"You're mine," she choked out.

And suddenly, just like a switch had been flipped, she saw her course stretched out before her. A slightly bigger home with space enough for her to create her flowers for clients. And her own wedding chapel overflowing with flower arches and the combination of flowers she loved.

She took his hands and brought them to her lips, kissing both the real and his new one. Looking into his eyes, she said, "And they lived happily ever after."

A grin spread over his ruggedly handsome features and his eyes glimmered with love. "It's only the beginning."

Epilogue

"Matthew Jeremy Rock, you come back here and get your life jacket!" Lexi called after the tan little boy sprinting out the cabin door away from her. Before she could even scream, her son took a running jump and cannonballed right into the bayou.

"Go after him!" she cried, but her husband was already on it, jumping in after their naughty son and swimming quickly to the boy, who seemed to be holding his own keeping his head above water.

By the time her husband lifted the child over the dock for Lexi to grab—and shake for scaring her, and in her hugely pregnant state too—Matt Jr. was spitting out a mouthful of water around a huge grin.

"God, he's going to scare me to death one of these days," she said as her husband hauled himself onto the dock too.

He reached for the boy and sat him down in his lap.

"Give him hell, Rocko," called out Chaz, who was just emerging from the cabin.

Matthew shot her brother a grin and proceeded to talk to their three-year-old son about water safety—and the importance of not sending his mother into labor because Matty''s little sister still had a few days till it was time for her to come out.

Except...

The tight squeezing pressure cinching her middle told her that might have actually done the trick in getting this girl out of her womb. At a projected ten pounds, the doctor was concerned a woman as small as Lexi wouldn't be able to have a natural birth, but the entire family had bets going on who was more stubborn — mom or daughter.

"Babe?"

He looked up at her.

"I appreciate you trying to impart some semblance of fear into that boy, but he takes after his father in being a daredevil and it won't matter what you say. I think it's time."

He blinked at her. "Time to say something to him? I'm trying to."

"I mean *time*."

Everyone around her froze and then suddenly there was a commotion. Sisters-in-law running back into the cabin for her bag and the guys reaching for the satellite phone at the same time.

She held up a hand. "I don't need a phone right now. I need my body in that canoe and my husband paddling us out of this bayou."

Matthew was on his feet, their son by the hand. "Here, squirt, you go with *Grand-mère*. Momma and I are going to the hospital right now."

Their son looked up at each of them, his eyes, just like Matthew's, round. "The hospital?"

She squatted. Maybe that wasn't such a good idea. Ohhh, the pressure. With her luck she'd birth this child on the deck of the family cabin in the middle of nowhere. She stood again and her husband lifted the boy so he was on eye level with her.

She cupped his precious little face, suddenly emotional. When she saw him again, she'd put his baby sister into his arms. He'd be a brand new brother.

"Remember how I said when it's time for the baby to be born, we will go to the hospital?"

"The baby's being borned?" he said.

"Yep. So you be good for *Grand-mère* and promise you won't try to jump off that dock again."

He turned his head to look at the water. "I wanna swim."

"Then you'll do it with your uncles or *Grand-père*. Understand?"

He bobbed his head. Then Lexi threw her arms around both of her men. The three of them bent their heads together and she smiled. At that moment, another pain hit, this one stronger.

Straightening, she announced, "All right. We'd better hit the canoe if we're getting to the hospital on time." People flurried around her, embracing her, and Matthew aided her into the canoe, which was loaded with their bags. Her hospital bag was in the trunk of the car, packed and ready for weeks now. Somehow, she'd just known this trip to the cabin might send her over the edge.

As Matthew pushed off from the dock and paddled like their lives depended on it, he caught her staring at him.

His face changed, showing her the vulnerable side she rarely glimpsed and only when he was bursting with emotion—the day they'd taken their wedding vows, when she'd told him she was pregnant the first time and again on the day of Matty's birth.

"You all right, baby doll?" His voice was rough.

She nodded and reached for his hand. "Perfect. Thank you for the gift."

He glanced at her rounded abdomen. "You're welcome, but you did all the work carrying her—"

She stopped him. "I don't mean Janey," she referred to their daughter who was soon to meet her parents. "I mean every day. Each day with you is a gift. I love you."

Leaning forward, he pressed his forehead against hers again and palmed her belly. "You and our family are my whole world. But damn, your stomach's rock hard."

"It is. Matthew?"

"Yeah, my love?"

"Better paddle fast."

READ ON FOR A SNEAK PEEK OF AT CLOSE RANGE, RANGER OPS BOOK 1\
Chapter One

"Good morning, sir."

"It's afternoon, Ranger Lieutenant."

Nash Sullivan had seen the sun rise two days and set two nights. He didn't know if he was even still on his feet let alone what numbers the hands on the clock pointed to.

He stood at attention before his superior officer, Colonel Robert Downs, Defense Coordinating Officer on the case Nash had just completed. The blinds were half drawn in the room, allowing the sunlight to slant across the table. It played with Nash's eyes, sending visions of the shadows made by chopper blades over the baked earth through his mind.

"Go on, Sullivan. Give your report."

"Sir, I am Ranger Lieutenant Nash Sullivan of Rangers Company A. My team consisted of nine other men sent to neutralize the threat along the Sabine River. Do you want me to name my team members, sir?"

"No, I know who they are. Just give your statement, Ranger Lieutenant." Nash's superior wasn't a man he knew well—only knew *of*. The stuff of legends, a decorated Texas Ranger who served a decade before his promotion to an advisor to the US military. And how he'd come to take interest in what was a relatively small threat in the US was a question mark in Nash's mind. After a grueling two-day battle, though, he may not be thinking straight.

Nash continued, "We arrived at O-four-hundred. It was still dark. I ordered my guys to split into teams of two and surround the building, which was a metal garage, sir. We didn't hear any noises and slipped in without detection."

As he spoke, the story came in spurts as he relived some of the moments before the words came to his mind. Basically, what he relayed to Downs was a clusterfuck. A raid that didn't stand a chance against the twenty-two terrorists holed up in that fucking garage—yet somehow Nash and his men had pulled out a Hail-Mary and done their jobs.

He didn't express how damn lucky they all were to walk away with their lives and only some minor cuts and scrapes among them—he only stated facts. That they had rooted out the guys in the garage, taken heavy fire, returned it and he himself had killed at least four of those bastards. His partner, Shaw Woodward, or Woody had taken down more. With his sharpshooter skills, the man was priceless as far as sidekicks went. If Nash was ever called upon for a duty like this again, he'd want Woody on his six.

When he finished speaking, Downs did not move or even twitch an eyebrow. He simply stared at Nash.

"That's all, sir."

"I see. Ranger Lieutenant Sullivan, have you ever been called on within Company A to handle a threat of his magnitude before?"

"Not quite like this, sir, but I've dealt with some shit in my days with the SWAT team."

The man didn't take offense to Nash cussin', which was a relief. He was too dead on his feet to guard his tongue, but Downs had led men before and knew their vocabulary consisted of the words fuck, hell, move and now.

Downs templed his fingers and contemplated Nash. He bore the scrutiny, prepared for any feedback on how he had led his team, good or bad. He'd made choices out there—some not so great—but none of his men were in body bags, so he wasn't going to apologize.

And if he did have issues with how Nash had handled things, well, he'd heard it before, that his temper took things too far and he needed to restrain himself. Hell, even his own brother said the same, and he'd gotten himself in a world of trouble nobody could help him out of.

Nash's shoulders ached. He hadn't sat down in hours and didn't know when he would again, at this rate. His mind was still laser-sharp, though. Nothing else mattered.

Just as he began to think Downs was just fucking with him, the man cleared his throat. He ran his hand through his high-and-tight haircut that was peppered with gray.

Nash waited.

"I don't often run across people I am impressed with, Sullivan."

"Sir."

"But I've seen Army Rangers fuck up missions like this, while you took nine men and got them into a position to take down those bastards. You realize the number of explosives we found on that property was enough to leave a big crater in the South."

"Yes, sir."

"From my standpoint, you are a bigger asset to the country than your role as a Texas Ranger allows you. And it just so happens that I have a job for you."

Nash's heart kicked up. "Whatever it is, sir, I hope I can get some sleep first."

He chuckled, eyeing him up. "I think a few hours can be arranged, but there's a unit forming right as we speak. If you're up for the challenge, I plan to send you and some of the men you fought with the past two days to Mexico."

Nash might have grinned if he had the energy. "I'd be honored, sir. Challenge accepted."

"Good." He stood and faced Nash. "Welcome to Operation Freedom Flag."

Nash straightened. "Operation Freedom Flag, the division of Homeland Security, sir?"

"The very one. You may have heard of a special ops unit operating in the South."

Knights Ops was known everywhere, though the team were like shadows, legends that nobody knew the real details of.

"Congratulations, Sullivan. You'll be leading Ranger Ops into Mexico. Do your country proud, Captain. Now go grab some rest. You deploy at O-six-hundred."

Nash reeled with all this information dumped into his tired mind. All he could do was thank Downs and take his leave. Once in the hallway, he stopped and stared at the wall for a moment.

Down the hall, a door opened and one of his guys walked out, looking similarly dazed.

Nash headed for him. "Linc."

Looking the worse for wear, with several abrasions down his face, where he'd obviously skidded on some rough ground, and sporting a crisscross of butterfly bandage strips above his left brow, Lincoln had likely never seen that kind of action as a Ranger investigating petty thefts.

He'd held his own, though, and Nash was damn proud to serve with him.

Linc lifted a hand and scratched at his head. "I don't rightly know what just happened in that debriefing."

Nash watched him closely. "Were you told to get some rest because you're hitting the ground running again in a few hours?"

He nodded. Suddenly, a big grin hit his face. "Do you think we're all going? Are we all part of Operation Freedom Flag now?"

Nash started to reply that he didn't know when Woody approached. Fatigue hadn't taken the cockiness out of Shaw's walk as he strutted toward them like he wore cowboy boots and a Stetson rather than tactical hard-soled boots and camo.

He shot them both a grin. "So... OFFSUS." The anagram stood for Operation Freedom Flag Southern US division, and Nash had never in a million years expected to become part of it.

Linc shook his head. "Hold up. Don't tell me they're calling Texas the South. It's the West."

Nash groaned. "You're not one of those guys who argues where we belong on the map, are ya? But yeah, you too, Woody?"

"Yep," Woody drawled.

Nash slapped him on the back, and Linc grabbed Woody's hand in a bro-grip. The trio stood there speaking quietly, when another door opened. A guy they'd just fought with emerged, slump-shouldered.

When he turned and walked the other direction, Nash watched him go.

"I don't think he's in," Linc said.

"He didn't handle that last shot well. Did you see him curled up in the corner like a bug?" Nash shifted his weight on his tired legs. "He's cut out to be a Texas Ranger, dealing with drugs, illegals and human trafficking. Now it seems like we're facing something altogether different." The motto of 'One Riot, One Ranger' didn't seem right in this case.

"What is it the Knight Ops say? Guts and glory one mission at a time." Woody's words fell over the three of them. They stood in silence for a moment, and Nash was finally sucking in the enormity of his sudden shift in career paths. When he'd watched the sun rise over the land, he'd been a Texas Ranger and damn proud of it.

Now he was a special ops force protecting his country. A captain.

"Damn, I must have charmed the hell out of Downs."

"Shit, you debriefed to Downs and impressed *him*? He's got brass balls, I hear." Linc raised his brows.

Woody just peered down at Nash's knees until he looked himself to see what was there.

"What is it?" Nash asked.

"Just checking if you wore a hole in those cammies after giving Downs all that head."

Nash burst out laughing and reached out to cuff his new buddy. Finally, three other teammates joined them in the hall, all appearing as stunned as Nash felt upon first hearing their new status.

Looking from face to face, Nash's chest swelled with what could only be pride. He stuck out his fist into the center of the circle. "Looks like we've got our six. Guts and glory—"

"One mission at a time," they finished with him.

GET YOUR COPY OF AT CLOSE RANGE ON AMAZON

Em Petrova

Em Petrova was raised by hippies in the wilds of Pennsylvania but told her parents at the age of four she wanted to be a gypsy when she grew up. She has a soft spot for babies, puppies and 90s Grunge music and believes in Bigfoot and aliens. She started writing at the age of twelve and prides herself on making her characters larger than life and her sex scenes hotter than hot.

She burst into the world of publishing in 2010 after having five beautiful bambinos and figuring they were old enough to get their own snacks while she pounds away at the keys. In her not-so-spare time, she is fur-mommy to a Labradoodle named Daisy Hasselhoff and works as editor with USA Today and New York Times bestselling authors.

Find Em Petrova at empetrova.com

Other Indie Titles by Em Petrova

West Protection
HIGH-STAKES COWBOY
RESCUED BY THE COWBOY
GUARDED BY THE COWBOY
COWBOY CONSPIRACY THEORY
COWBOY IN THE CORSSHAIRS
PROTECTED BY THE COWBOY

Xtreme Ops
HITTING XTREMES
TO THE XTREME
XTREME BEHAVIOR
XTREME AFFAIRS
XTREME MEASURES
XTREME PRESSURE
XTREME LIMITS
Xtreme Ops Alaska Search and Rescue
NORTH OF LOVE

Crossroads
BAD IN BOOTS
CONFIDENT IN CHAPS
COCKY IN A COWBOY HAT

SAVAGE IN A STETSON
SHOW-OFF IN SPURS

Dark Falcons MC
DIXON
TANK
PATRIOT
DIESEL
BLADE

The Guard
HIS TO SHELTER
HIS TO DEFEND
HIS TO PROTECT

Moon Ranch
TOUGH AND TAMED
SCREWED AND SATISFIED
CHISELED AND CLAIMED

Ranger Ops
AT CLOSE RANGE
WITHIN RANGE
POINT BLANK RANGE
RANGE OF MOTION
TARGET IN RANGE

214

OUT OF RANGE

Knight Ops Series
ALL KNIGHTER
HEAT OF THE KNIGHT
HOT LOUISIANA KNIGHT
AFTER MIDKNIGHT
KNIGHT SHIFT
ANGEL OF THE KNIGHT
O CHRISTMAS KNIGHT

Wild West Series
SOMETHING ABOUT A LAWMAN
SOMETHING ABOUT A SHERIFF
SOMETHING ABOUT A BOUNTY HUNTER
SOMETHING ABOUT A MOUNTAIN MAN

Operation Cowboy Series
KICKIN' UP DUST
SPURS AND SURRENDER

The Boot Knockers Ranch Series
PUSHIN' BUTTONS
BODY LANGUAGE
REINING MEN
ROPIN' HEARTS

ROPE BURN
COWBOY NOT INCLUDED
COWBOY BY CANDLELIGHT
THE BOOT KNOCKER'S BABY
ROPIN' A ROMEO
WINNING WYOMING

Ménage à Trouble Series
WRANGLED UP
UP FOR GRABS
HOOKING UP
ALL WOUND UP
DOUBLED UP novella duet
UP CLOSE
WARMED UP

Another Shot at Love Series
GRIFFIN
BRANT
AXEL

Rope 'n Ride Series
BUCK
RYDER
RIDGE
WEST

216

LANE
WYNONNA

The Dalton Boys
COWBOY CRAZY Hank's story
COWBOY BARGAIN Cash's story
COWBOY CRUSHIN' Witt's story
COWBOY SECRET Beck's story
COWBOY RUSH Kade's Story
COWBOY MISTLETOE a Christmas novella
COWBOY FLIRTATION Ford's story
COWBOY TEMPTATION Easton's story
COWBOY SURPRISE Justus's story
COWGIRL DREAMER Gracie's story
COWGIRL MIRACLE Jessamine's story
COWGIRL HEART Kezziah's story

Single Titles and Boxes
THE BOOT KNOCKERS RANCH BOX SET
THE DALTON BOYS BOX SET
SINFUL HEARTS
JINGLE BOOTS
A COWBOY FOR CHRISTMAS
FULL RIDE

Club Ties Series

LOVE TIES
HEART TIES
MARKED AS HIS
SOUL TIES
ACE'S WILD

Firehouse 5 Series
ONE FIERY NIGHT
CONTROLLED BURN
SMOLDERING HEARTS

Hardworking Heroes Novellas
STRANDED AND STRADDLED
DALLAS NIGHTS
SLICK RIDER
SPURRED ON